ALIEN
SECRETS

ALIEN
SECRETS

ANNETTE CURTIS KLAUSE

A YEARLING BOOK

Published by
Bantam Doubleday Dell Books for Young Readers
a division of
Bantam Doubleday Dell Publishing Group, Inc.
1540 Broadway
New York, New York 10036

The trademark Yearling® is registered in the
U.S. Patent and Trademark Office.

The trademark Dell® is registered in the
U.S. Patent and Trademark Office.

ISBN: 0-440-41061-4

Reprinted by arrangement with Delacorte Press
Printed in the United States of America
January 1995
10   9   8   7   6   5   4   3   2
OPM

To Daddy,
who showed me the way
to the stars;
and Mark,
who travels there with me.

Puck: *My fairy lord, this must be done with haste,*
For night's swift dragons cut the clouds full fast,
And yonder shines Aurora's harbinger;
At whose approach ghosts, wand'ring here and there,
Troop home to churchyards; damnèd spirits all,
That in crossways and floods have burial,
Already to their wormy beds are gone.
For fear lest day should look their shames upon,
They willfully themselves exile from light,
And must for aye consort with black-browed night.

—WILLIAM SHAKESPEARE,
A Midsummer Night's Dream,
Act III, Scene ii.

Puck was exploring the back end of the spaceport docks when she ran smack into the fight.

Two men were locked in a frantic struggle in the half-light of a disused bay. The taller, leaner of the two broke free and slugged his stocky, bearded foe in the mouth. The other man staggered, giving the tall man time to gather a throttling grip on the neck of his shirt.

"Where is it, Bean?" the tall man growled.

Bean choked, spittle flecking his dark beard. Puck was terrified to see him slide a lightknife from the back of his waistband and flick on the deadly vibrating laser blade. He swung it around viciously, but the tall man saw and leapt back, pushing Bean off balance. He brought his foot up in a crushing blow to Bean's groin. Bean crumpled and dropped the lightknife. The tall man snatched it up before it hit the ground and was on his opponent almost as soon as he'd caught it, holding the weapon close to Bean's throat. A red line traveled Bean's neck, and he whimpered in fear.

Puck inched away, the smell of singed beard in her nostrils, but panic made her numb and clumsy. She backed into a packing crate and yelped.

The tall man looked up, and Puck stared into a pair of cold blue eyes.

Oh, God, she thought. *He knows I'm here.*

She broke free and ran—ran as fast as she could, back to the safety of the passenger lounge, back to light and people and reality. In the morning she'd be on a ship. She'd be on her way, and she'd never see him again.

But all the way back to the everyday silver corridors, she imagined the slice of the knife in her back.

CHAPTER
ONE

"There's the alien," an excited voice whispered.

Puck instantly turned from the viewport and looked around. Nearby was an overweight, grandmotherly type with large, bubbly earrings, and a taller, severe-looking woman, with dark, close-cropped hair.

The dark-haired one tugged at the arm of her companion. "Over there," she said, "Can you believe it?"

Puck glanced before she could stop herself. A lanky humanoid creature in a black robe stood at the other end of the viewport. Absolute zero! Her first alien, and they hadn't even taken off.

Aliens weren't allowed on Earth yet, even as diplomats; after all, to be blown out of the sky by a Grakk cruiser wasn't exactly the most encouraging first contact, and the twenty-year war that followed hadn't made anyone eager to be friends with nonhumans.

This wasn't a Grakk, though, or any of the others she'd seen in the vids. Of course, since the Peace a lot more kinds of aliens were surfacing than anyone had suspected. The Grakk had a nasty habit of capturing slaves to do their dirty work. Unfortunately some people lumped all alien peoples into the same category with the Grakk and called them Bug-Eyed Monsters, or bemmies for short.

I bet the Peace Committee's getting a real headache trying to figure out where everyone belongs, Puck thought. Maybe this alien was one of their projects.

She wondered if the alien had been as dismayed as she was when they announced the twenty-four-hour delay in boarding. She'd barely slept last night, terrified that she'd run into that man with the knife before she left the orbiting space station. Time and again she'd almost gone to the station master's office to report the fight, but held back because then she'd have to explain why she'd been in a restricted area. Anyhow she didn't know if Bean had actually been killed, did she? Except there were blue-suits all over today—police swarming the way they did when there was trouble.

The alien stared out the viewport, but his large eyes seemed glazed. Was he daydreaming? Alien expressions were probably completely different from human ones. Although he was about a foot taller than most human men, and thinner, he did look almost human except for his long pointed head and his skin, which was gray and slightly wrinkled like an elephant's. He clutched a pendant at his neck with elongated, knobby fingers. Instead of a little finger, he had another thumb. Puck realized she was staring and averted her eyes.

The elderly women appeared to be arguing. Puck sidled closer to hear what they were talking about, and her movement caught the attention of the plump one.

"Do not make a fuss," the plump woman said.

"Well, he certainly made a fuss on the station, why's he so quiet now?" the dark-haired woman replied. Then she saw Puck too.

Puck blushed.

The dark-haired woman nodded curtly, but the plump one advanced on Puck in a cloud of perfume, her earrings jiggling. "Hello, my dear," she gushed in a fruity voice. "It is exciting traveling by spaceship, is it not? Is this your first time?" Half her face didn't work quite right, as if she'd had a stroke or something.

She was the sort of person who stood much too close, and Puck had to try hard not to be rude and back away. "Yes, Mz. It's my first time," she lied to avoid explaining.

"Oh my, how thrilling for you."

Puck attempted to smile.

"I am Beatrice Florette," the woman said, "and my companion here is Mz Antonia Dante. What a yum child, is she not, Antonia? What lovely red curls."

Puck almost winced. No one used *yum* anymore.

"You must introduce us to your parents, dear."

"I'm sorry," Puck said. "I'm traveling alone."

"Alone! A child like you?"

Puck drew herself up to her full five foot one. "I'm almost thirteen," she said, and some of her indignation must have slipped through, because the woman giggled nervously.

"Well, well. Traveling alone. How clever. And where are you going?"

"Aurora. My parents work there."

"Oh, how lovely," the plump woman said. "That is where we are going. Antonia has a job on that world."

Puck wondered what Mz Dante's job could be. She didn't seem the type who had to work; she wore quietly expensive clothes and jewelry that looked like those worn by the elegant mothers of some of Puck's rich school friends.

"Going home for the vacation, are you?" Mz Dante said.

Puck crossed her fingers behind her back. "Yeah."

"Only one stop between here and there," the plump woman said. "Not a bad leap."

"Let the girl alone, Beat," the dark-haired woman said in an exasperated tone. "She's not in the mood to talk." Puck was relieved. Mz Dante looked a bit strict, but maybe she was all right.

"We will leave you to your view, then, Mz . . . ?"

"Oh, sorry," Puck said. "Robin Goodfellow."

"Indeed?" Mz Dante's lips curved briefly. " 'Either I mistake your shape and making quite, or else you are that shrewd and knavish sprite called Robin Goodfellow.' "

Puck rolled her eyes.

"Shakespeare," Mz Dante said. *"A Midsummer Night's Dream."*

"Yeah," Puck answered. "I know." She found it irritating that her parents had given her a name that caused people to compulsively quote lines at her. Still, she liked the nickname that went with it—Robin Goodfellow was also known as Puck—but she wasn't sure being named after a mischievous elf was good luck. It's probably what stunted my growth, she'd told Gran.

Mz Dante didn't push the issue. "Well, Mz Goodfellow, if you need any help on your journey, don't hesitate to ask."

"Oh, yes do," said Mz Florette putting her white, doughy hands on Puck's shoulders. "Do, please." Puck was afraid for a moment that the soppy woman was going to kiss her.

But Mz Dante interrupted. "Come along, Beat."

Mz Dante firmly led the way, and Mz Florette hurried after, her tight plastisuit making her flesh bunch and unbunch in repulsive lumps. Puck repressed a giggle.

Puck turned to have another look at the alien. He pulled a long, velvety black pouch from the inner folds of his robe. Solemnly he turned it inside out and inspected the seams, then he shoved it back beneath his robe. His other hand clenched tight and beat slowly and fiercely against his thigh.

Before she could figure that out, a fluting whistle filled the air. Two gray-clad officers entered the lounge, followed by a young man in coveralls who looked about college age. Each had a patch on one shoulder—an insignia composed of a cat and stars. Puck joined the other passengers gathered in front of them. Everyone had bits and pieces of hand luggage except Mz Dante and Mz Florette. *I'll bet they already had someone carry everything to their cabins,* she thought. They appeared to be accustomed to being pampered.

Besides the two ladies and Puck, there was a young couple, and a tall man in conservative ankle-tie baggies who must have just arrived—six travelers in all, plus the alien, who hung back a little behind the group. Whenever she dared glance at him, he was staring intently at one or another of the passengers. *Well,* she thought, *we're strange to him too.*

"Welcome aboard *Cat's Cradle,*" said a sturdy woman in dark gray knee-length pantlettes and a short jacket to match. The whispers died away. "I am your captain, Louise Biko."

Her complexion was warm brown, her curls crisp and dark, and her cheeks full. She moved and spoke efficiently, but there were lines around her eyes and mouth in the places a face would crinkle when someone laughed. Puck imagined that laugh would be as deep and rich as her speaking voice.

The captain introduced the people with her. The young man was called Michael Tse. Puck liked his grin.

"I'm sorry for the delay," Captain Biko said, "but as you know, we were not expecting so many passengers until the *Star Queen* developed engine trouble."

Puck wondered if she'd been the only passenger booked on *Cat's Cradle* to begin with. Everyone else looked like they could afford a star liner.

"Excuse me, Captain?" The tall man stepped forward,

and Puck studied his back. His shoulders were broad, his hips lean. He wore a small gold earring like men from Paradise often did. "Is there any truth to the rumor I heard that the damage to the *Star Queen*'s stellar drive was sabotage?" he asked.

"I'm afraid I can't answer that, Mizzer Cubuk. All I know is that this is a chance to make some extra credits, begging your pardon."

There were a few laughs.

"Thank you, Captain," said Mizzer Cubuk. "Just trying to identify the mysterious forces that have allowed me the pleasure of flying on your ship again."

Captain Biko's face creased into exactly the smile Puck had expected. "The forces of good, no doubt. Welcome aboard once more, Tee."

The young woman next to Puck whispered excitedly to her male companion. He whispered back, sounding annoyed.

"We will be doing a circuit run," the captain continued. "Jackpot, Aurora, Uy Ceti, Paradise, Barnard's Star, then home. Meals will be taken with the crew in the mess hall, and you are welcome to use the entertainments in this lounge for recreation. Access to other parts of the ship will be limited. We are primarily a freighter, not a passenger ship. After lift-off, however, we may be able to arrange a tour. If there are no questions, I will assign you an escort to your room."

She paused briefly, but no one spoke up. "The tugs have

hooked up, and the station pilot is about to maneuver us out into clear space. Once in your cabins, please strap into your couches and stay restrained until you hear the all-clear. This will sound when we have made a roll into the correct trajectory, and the system drive has kicked in. You will find a container under your seat in case you experience discomfort. Thank you."

As if waiting for this cue, a low-pitched whine began by the window, and the view of the spaceport was gradually obliterated by a descending segment of the outer hull.

A blond officer approached Mizzer Cubuk and beckoned also to the alien. Everyone turned to watch the alien glide forward as if through water, his head turning gently from side to side, slightly bobbing. His eyes weren't glazed now, they were large and dark. Puck was sure he was frightened, he looked so solemn.

Puck stepped slowly aside as he approached so that she wouldn't startle him. Mz Dante also slid away gracefully, but Mz Florette didn't catch on, and the edge of the alien's robe brushed her knee. She yelped and jerked back. The alien flinched and stopped. For a moment they stared at each other. The alien's small nose twitched like a rabbit's, and Mz Florette appeared to be holding her breath. Then, with dignity, the alien bowed to her as if apologizing and continued through. He carefully avoided touching anyone else as he went.

Mizzer Cubuk came forward to greet the alien. Cubuk had a chiseled face that made him look strong and deter-

mined, and—Puck's mouth went dry—pale blue eyes. He
was the man in the fight. Was he following her? She edged
backward, but he didn't even glance her way. She'd been
in the shadows during the fight. Maybe he hadn't seen her
properly.

"Wake up," said an amused voice beside her. She inhaled sharply.

"Sorry, didn't mean to startle you." The young man
who had entered with the officers stood beside her. He
had a wide olive face and eyes like an elven prince.

"You're Michael, aren't you?" she said, wishing she
hadn't jumped.

"Yeah, acting as steward right now. I'm supposed to take
you and the young lovers to your cabins."

"Great." Puck hoped she sounded enthusiastic. She
tried to dismiss Cubuk from her thoughts. He'd been on a
spaceport, for Earth's sake, so chances were he was planning on taking a ship somewhere. Why not this one? She'd
have to keep out of his way, that's all. "My name's Puck,"
she said.

The couple had wandered off to a couch to read a
hardcopy print from a news vid. They both had thick, pale
hair, the man's longer than was fashionable. The woman
wore hers loose and wild.

"Another Grakk storehouse was broken into this week,"
the man was saying as Puck and Michael walked up. "This
time on Ledo." He had a lazy drawl, near laughter.

11

"It's a bit of a nerve calling it theft, isn't it," the woman answered, "considering it's all stolen to begin with."

" 'The plundered wealth of alien nations,' Murphy calls it," the man said.

She laughed. "That does sound like Murphy."

Michael cleared his throat, and the man looked up. "Hi ho! You must be here to escort us. Come on, heart." He pulled the woman from her seat.

Puck walked ahead with Michael. She wanted to ask if he knew anything about Cubuk, but that seemed too much like tempting fate. Instead she brought up that other passenger. "It's great, isn't it, having an alien on board."

"Yeah, real," Michael answered.

"Where's he going?" she asked.

"Aurora."

"That's where I'm going," she squeaked in surprise. "One of those women said he made a fuss on the station."

"Oh, that," Michael said eagerly. "From what I heard, something of his was stolen on Earth Station, and they were afraid he'd refuse to leave. That made a lot of people nervous. They want to get him home safely to keep on his people's good side."

"Yike!" Puck said. She remembered the bag he'd held and the sad way he'd looked at it.

"That old lady was really bothered by the alien, wasn't she," Michael said.

"Yeah, really."

Michael laughed. "Wait till she hears some of the strange stories about this ship."

"What?"

"Tell you later," Michael said, tilting his head meaningfully toward an officer who stood by the lift.

CHAPTER
TWO

The all-clear throbbed to an end.

"Whoosh!" Puck sighed. She flipped the catch on the shoulder strap and found the button that eased her to a sitting position.

She felt safe locked in her cabin. No one could get in unless she said so—especially that Mizzer Cubuk. The room smelled fresh, and everything was creamy green and rounded off. Even the ceiling was domed. It wasn't anything like she'd anticipated. Then again, the outside of the ship didn't look anything like the sturdy ribbed bullets she used to ride with her parents either; it looked more like a beehive.

There was a peephole in the door, above the list of emergency procedures. She didn't expect to see anyone when she looked out, so her eyes widened when she saw the alien.

He was leaning his domed head against the corridor wall opposite her room, the wall that wrapped around the ship's core and contained the lifts. He held the thing he wore around his neck up to the matte metallic finish with his spidery fingers and stood motionless, eyes closed.

Then a chime sounded in the corridor, announcing the opening of the passenger lift. He snatched his pendant to him, turned in a swirl of dark robes, and hurried away from the approaching laughter in his strange, bobbing gait.

Wow. She pulled reluctantly away from the door. Should she report this to the captain? But the idea of telling on someone made her stomach squirm. *Give the guy a break,* she thought, as she emptied her suitcase. What did she know about how aliens behaved? Maybe this was normal. *I think I'll keep an eye on him, though,* she decided, bunching up her jumpsuits and unitards to fit clumsily into a chest of drawers. He was much too interesting to ignore.

A soft bell from the direction of the desk made her jump. She turned to see a message alert hovering over a vidcom grid. "Dinner at 1800," the vidcom said in an impersonal contralto voice when she prompted it, and then it projected a color-coded map to show her the way. Two whole hours away. Her stomach growled.

As she reached to turn the message off, she could feel the crackling of the clumsily folded printout that hid in her breast pocket—her parents' last relay communication. "Looking forward to seeing you," the com said. Yeah, but they would have preferred it to be a year from now, when they were settled in, not a week. They hadn't counted on her getting expelled.

It was so dumb. All the trouble she'd gotten into at that school, and she was finally tossed out for something as simple as bad grades. Her parents, the scientific geniuses who already talked about her joining their team, were probably looking forward to seeing her so that they could yell.

Hey, she told herself. *It's been so long since they've seen me, they won't recognize me. I'll slip by them and escape.* But the idea of them not recognizing her brought tears to her eyes. *Stupid,* she thought. *I'm just tired.*

"Help," she said, and suddenly a menu of data banks and programs hovered in front of her.

She laughed. "That's not what I meant." But since the vidcom offered, she requested the encyclopedia and asked for the read option. Having machines talk to her bothered her slightly; they usually spoke with adult voices.

"Word search—Aurora, planet," she said, and the vidcom complied. But there was nothing she didn't know.

Second planet of Tau Ceti, she read. *A G type, yellow-white main-sequence star of 3.5 magnitude and 0.9 solar mass, 11.7 light-years from Earth. The planet is known for its spectacular sunsets and sunrises due to the level of meteor dust in the upper atmosphere. Native name: Shoon.*

Until the end of the war Aurora had been occupied by the Grakk, who used the natives as technical labor and to produce food for the larger, sister planet the Grakk preferred—it had heavier gravity and plenty of carbon dioxide. They had also used Aurora to train their troops to fight in an Earth-like atmosphere.

There were cross-references to *Shoowa, Grakk,* and *Tau Ceti.* The *Shoowa* entry began with an explanation that *their*

16

technology is well disguised within their agrarian society, so that the advanced level of their prestarflight civilization is not apparent at first. She stopped reading that pretty fast. Boring. The picture was exactly like that alien, though.

She didn't bother with the *Grakk* entry. Most of them had fled after the war, and the few captured ones had curled up and gone into hibernation. But you only had to watch the old war-story vids to know the Grakk were squat, smelly, frog-faced creatures with vicious tempers and a language that made them sound as if they had something stuck in their throat. They had come from an old star nearer the center of the galaxy when it threatened to go nova, and while they were looking for a star to replace it, they got a taste for collecting planets and slaves. They'd first clashed with Terrans when they'd both been checking out Epsilon Eridani.

Puck dumped the contents of her carrier on the couch and rediscovered the bars of chocolate that Gran had given her for the trip. Then she pulled two light-frames from the jumble and slid them into the grips on the desk top next to the vidcom. The holographic figures seemed to hover on the brink of movement. Gran was plump and small in her favorite dark blue robe with the hood. She was dancing in the kitchen on Christmas morning. *I'm going to miss you, Gran,* Puck thought.

Puck's parents stood in front of some government-issue hut on a planet called Smith's Luck that Puck had seen only in this photo. They smiled and waved as if she were coming down the path toward them. When she thought of them, it was this picture she saw, the real memories were so faded.

The old familiar anger rose easily. Why did they have to leave her with Gran? Why couldn't they have taken her with them? Wasn't travel supposed to be educational? If they were so concerned about her getting a good education, they could have taught her. They were the ones with all the degrees. What made them think an Earthside school could teach her better than they could?

Except maybe now she'd miss that school.

She pulled a picture from another of her overall pockets, a cheap threedee photo with curling edges. Her best friend, Naima Singh, had ducked into one of those machines at the train station and had it taken moments before the bullet to London arrived. Puck tucked it into the frame of her grandmother's picture. There were no kids on Aurora.

A crumpled card signed by her classmates was hidden under her grafix-screen. She carefully smoothed the creases. Who would have thought she would have made friends at Stonebrook—an all-girl, English boarding school, for crying out loud. She'd nearly died when Gran told her about it. "I went there as a girl," Gran had said. "It'll give you some discipline. You're running wild here with me."

A knock at the door startled Puck. But when she forced

herself to look through the peephole, it wasn't Cubuk she saw. She was surprised to find the captain outside.

"Yes, Mz?" she said, opening the door. She should have been more relieved, but she couldn't help remembering that the captain was friends with Cubuk.

"I see you're settling in," the captain said as she came through the door. She noticed the chocolate. "May I? I love chocolate."

"Sure," Puck said, awed by her powerful guest.

"I need your help," Captain Biko said, licking her fingers and perching on the edge of Puck's couch. "As you've realized, we have a passenger aboard who's not from Earth. He's one of a group of Shoowa who were held as slaves by the Grakk for several generations. He's the first of his people to travel home."

"To Aurora," Puck said.

The captain nodded. "He's had a rough time lately."

Puck remembered what Michael had said about the stolen whatever.

"He's a little frightened and shy," continued the captain. "I think it would be wonderful if he could find a friend."

"A friend?" Puck echoed.

"I hope you don't mind me saying so, but I think that a child would be less threatening to him," the captain finished.

"You want me to make friends with the alien?" Puck asked without wiping the surprise from her voice.

The captain frowned slightly. "Would you find that distasteful?"

"No, no," Puck responded hastily. What a perfect opportunity to keep an eye on him. "But why?"

The captain laughed. It was a good laugh that lit up her face. "Lots of reasons, I suppose. I like people to be happy on my ship. I feel sorry for him. I'm angry that he was once enslaved. Maybe most of all, I've been a lonely stranger more than once myself."

"Me too," Puck said quietly, warming toward the woman. "Why didn't they give him an escort?" she asked.

"I heard he refused one," the captain answered. "He said he was a free person now and wanted to travel like one."

Puck knew how he felt. "But how do I get to know him?"

"I'll leave that up to you," said the captain. "You've made friends before, haven't you?"

Not easily, Puck thought. "Okay, Captain Biko," she said.

"Cat," said the captain. "Captain Cat, my friends call me."

"I'm Puck," Puck said before she could help it.

"I'm glad to know that," the captain said warmly.

Suddenly Puck wanted to trust the woman. *Should I warn her about Cubuk?* she thought. *Maybe she doesn't know him that well.* But Puck had no proof, and maybe the captain wouldn't like her after she'd spoken against him.

The captain took the lull in the conversation as an opportunity to leave. "I need to get back to my bridge."

After Captain Cat left, Puck returned to putting her things away. *I really don't know anything about it,* she decided. *Maybe Cubuk had a good reason to fight that man.* She pushed aside the memory of the knife, the red-streaked throat, and the only possible conclusion. *I'm not a coward, I'm sensible,* she told herself.

She grabbed her bath kit. *Why in heaven would this alien want to be friends with me?* she wondered. *I'm an ordinary kid and a screw-up at that.*

In the 'fresher was a real bath and shower, not one of those horrid mist things. There was even a retractable water-pick hose in the wall. They made great water pistols if you could get someone in range. She tried some experimental shots at the shower curtain, then rubbed her cheek admiringly against a cream towel. It was embossed with the ship's logo—a cat and stars.

Puck yawned. Her sleepless night was catching up with her fast. *Maybe I should slide back for a while,* she decided, heading for the couch. *I'm not going to think about aliens or anything. I'm going to relax.*

—

I refuse to wake up, Puck thought, and squeezed her eyes together. But a chorus of voices moaned outside her door like a choir struck by bellyache. They nagged her awake.

"I'll murder them," Puck growled, struggling to find the

light switch, which had mysteriously lost itself. "Stupid girls, playing tricks."

By accident she found the sensi-spot, and the lights bloomed. She squinted as her brain and eyes focused.

Oh, right, this wasn't school. But if that wasn't the girls . . .

Goosebumps rippled over her skin. What were those hideous noises? It sounded like banshees wailing outside.

The moaning that woke her rose to a bloodcurdling howl—then someone screamed.

CHAPTER
THREE

Puck slid off the couch and ran to the door. She stopped there for a second, heart pounding. Cautiously she looked through the peephole, but could see nothing.

There was silence now. It was almost worse than the moans.

"Mind your own business," Gran would say. But what if the scream had something to do with Cubuk? That would make it her business because she hadn't told. She smacked the release, and the door whisked open.

"Leesa!" a man cried.

Puck ducked her head out, looked right, looked left, and jerked back in.

What had she seen? Right—nothing; left—young blond couple, she on the ground, he falling to his knees. No monsters. No Cubuk.

Carefully Puck stepped across the threshold.

The woman was sobbing into the shoulder of her husband. An officer came running around the corridor from the direction of the lift, buttoning his gray jacket. "Someone reported a scream," he said as he stumbled to a halt. He smoothed back his thinning brown hair while he waited for an explanation. Around the curve of the passenger deck the others kept to themselves. Even the one who reported the scream stayed anonymous. He had done his duty.

The officer cleared his throat. "I'm William Ernest, the medical officer and second mate," he said. "Can I help?"

"Loki Sigmund," said the man on the floor. "I'm afraid Leesa's had a bit of a shock."

Mz. Sigmund wiped at her eyes with a fist. "It was awful," she said, her voice trembling on the edge of tears.

Mizzer Ernest's wristie beeped. "Never mind," he said into it. "I can handle things."

"Perhaps if you told me about it, we could set things straight," he said to the young woman hopefully. He bent toward her, resting his hands on his knees.

"I don't know. I'm not even sure it makes sense."

"Try me," he urged.

Puck edged closer.

Mz Sigmund took a deep breath. "I couldn't sleep. I decided to walk around the corridor a few times to get some exercise." She stopped, and looked about nervously.

"Yes?" prompted Mizzer Ernest gently.

"The lights started flickering, then they dimmed, and I suddenly felt very cold." She pulled her emerald-green robe closer around her, as if she felt the cold again. "Then there was a horrible noise. This shrieking and moaning."

"But I didn't hear anything," her husband said.

"I don't know how you couldn't," she snapped, then instantly looked sorry and touched his hand. "And then I felt there were people around me," she said to Mizzer Ernest.

"People? What do you mean 'people'?" Mizzer Ernest straightened up, shaking his head.

"How could you have felt people, heart?" her husband asked.

Mz Sigmund flushed, seeing his disbelief. "I don't know. The air around me felt occupied somehow. I felt crowded and claustrophobic. And the noise was terrible—like the cries of people tortured in hell."

The skin on Puck's back crawled as if someone were running ice-cold fingers down her spine. Those stories Michael mentioned must have been ghost stories.

"And that's when you screamed?" Mizzer Ernest asked.

Mz Sigmund swallowed visibly. "I screamed when something sliced me like a cold knife." Her voice rose in pitch. "One of them walked through me. I know it."

"Oh, Leesa." Loki Sigmund stroked her hair. "How could you know it was something walking through you?"

"Because for a moment I could hear the screaming right inside my head, and I didn't feel like me. I felt as if I would never do anything but cry again."

Mizzer Ernest cleared his throat again before he finally spoke. "Uh, you didn't take anything to help you sleep, did you?"

Mz Sigmund stiffened. "Are you suggesting I'm intoxicated?"

"Well, ah, no, no. Just a light sedative maybe," he trailed off.

"Leesa doesn't take sedatives," Mizzer Sigmund said firmly.

"Of course not," Mizzer Ernest rushed to agree. "But, um, sometimes, you know, people react strangely to space travel."

"Well, perhaps she's overtired," Mz Sigmund's husband allowed, speaking about her as if she were a child.

The men were infuriating. "But I heard the noises too," Puck said.

Both men turned abruptly at the sound of her voice.

"Well, young lady," Mizzer Ernest said, hand clutching his chest, "where did you come from?" He looked white as a sheet. Maybe Mz Sigmund's tale had got to him after all.

"I've been here all the time," Puck said.

"Sometimes the air vents make strange noises when we accelerate," Mizzer Ernest said. "They conduct sound up the ship from the engine room. I expect that's all you heard."

"That sounds reasonable," Mizzer Sigmund joined in, giving his wife a squeeze.

Yeah, right, Puck thought. She knew a brush-off when she heard one. And there was Leesa Sigmund nodding like she was starting to believe them. "That wasn't ship noises," Puck said angrily.

"Perhaps we had better continue this discussion in the morning," Mizzer Ernest said. "I'm sure everyone's ex-

tremely tired. Off to bed, young lady. Excitement's over."
He shooed her off with a motion of his hand.

But I did hear it, Puck thought, as she climbed back into
bed. First thugs, now ghosts. What kind of ship was this?
She found it hard to fall back to sleep.

—

Puck woke early despite her interrupted night. Underneath the time on her vidcom projection was an invitation
to breakfast, and she realized she was ravenous. Maybe
she'd see Michael in the mess hall. She could ask him
about the stories he'd mentioned. She just knew they had
to be about those strange noises. Maybe the alien would be
there, too, if he ate Earth food.

Bacon and eggs and biscuits, she wished hard as she left
her cabin. But she put a chocolate bar into her pocket in
case they only had synthetic stuff, then she walked the cir-
cular corridor the long way around to the passenger lift so
that she could explore.

Facing the second cabin along was a huge elevator,
much bigger than the one she had come down in. There
was a sign posted on its doors: FREIGHT ONLY. PASSENGERS
PLEASE USE OTHER LIFT.

Whoa, they must haul some giant stuff, Puck thought, then
her eyes caught a gentle movement near the floor. A tuft of
green material, trapped in the lift doors, fluttered in the
draft from a ventilation grate.

Puck wrinkled her forehead. Where had she seen that

color before? Then she remembered. It was the color of Leesa Sigmund's robe.

Mz Sigmund must have had that door open to get her robe caught. Maybe she'd even been riding on the lift. She hadn't told that officer the whole truth about what she'd been doing last night. What was she hiding?

CHAPTER
FOUR

Puck hesitated in the doorway of the mess hall until she noticed Michael sitting by himself. He looked up and smiled at her, and that was invitation enough; she went to join him.

"Through there," Michael said before she could ask, pointing to an archway. Chromed counters glistened beyond. "It's a short-hop trip—plenty of real food."

"Yay!" Puck said, and soon returned with a heaping plate of scrambled eggs, bacon, and toast, a pastry perched precariously on the side.

Michael laughed. "Are you sure you've got room for all that? I'd say you were a growing girl, but I've got my doubts."

Puck bristled. She couldn't help being small. There were plenty of girls at school who knew it didn't hold her back in a scrap.

"Hey! No offense," Michael exclaimed, so Puck calmed down. No sense in losing a possible friend by arguing.

"You're up early," he said.

"I zeed out early last night." Puck dug into her food.

"Yeah, I saw you weren't at dinner."

Puck felt a warm pleasure that he'd noticed. "You hear

about all that fuss last night?" she asked, dying to tell him if he hadn't.

He looked at her blankly. "What fuss? I just got up."

She gave him a rundown of what happened, delighted to see him look increasingly astonished. "Why do you think Mz Sigmund was in the freight lift?" she asked him, finally.

Michael shrugged. "Maybe she's nosy. I guess you never poke around new places, huh?"

Boy, he'd nailed her. "You believe me about the noises, don't you?" she asked.

He sipped his coffee while he thought about it. Of course he couldn't possibly be interested in someone as young as her, but Puck wished the girls could see her anyway.

"There have been stories," Michael began promisingly, and she leaned toward him. "But I don't see how she could have heard them, so they couldn't have influenced her."

"What stories, for sweet's sake?" Puck asked.

He set down his cup. "You're not the type to get scared easily, are you?"

"I'm no screamer," she said. There were scarier things than bumps in the night. Real people, for instance.

"We're not supposed to let on, since it's not good for business, and don't you dare let anyone know I told you. . . ." His voice lowered eagerly. "But people have heard strange noises in the freight holds, especially in the lower hold—groanings and moanings. And now and then, in hyperspace, someone sees a figure out of the corner of their eye—gray and wobbly." He paused, relishing the drama. "Some people say this ship is haunted."

Puck shivered. "Have you . . . ?"

"Tse!" a harsh voice spat, and Puck's words choked off. Michael snapped up straight in his seat.

An officer stood by their table. His middle-aged face seemed creased in a permanent frown, and his rigid back hinted at a lifetime devoted to posture. *They would have loved him at Stonebrook,* Puck thought.

"Don't you have a tour to conduct?" the officer said.

"Yes, sir."

"Well, get on with it, boy," the man growled, and marched smartly to the kitchen. The people he passed nodded dutifully to him.

"Mizzer Nast, the first mate," Michael said. "What a sweetheart."

"Yeah," she agreed.

Puck glanced around to see if anyone else had come in. She was disappointed that the alien hadn't shown up.

"Want to go on this tour?" Michael asked.

"Let me check my appointment book," she answered, following him to the corridor. "Those ghosts . . ."

"Not now," Michael told her.

Just then she saw Mizzer Cubuk coming toward them. This time he did notice her. His eyes narrowed and he stroked his chin. Puck dodged to the far side of Michael so that she could hide behind him, and urged him on with a tug at his arm. "So what do you do around here anyway?" she asked, her voice squeaking. "Besides conduct tours, that is." She looked back nervously, but Cubuk had walked on.

"I'm a student," Michael said, his voice filling with pride. "At the Merchant Spacers Academy, Star Point. Top five percent of my class."

"Then what are you doing working on this crate hauler?" Tension made her sound more rude than teasing.

"It's my internship," he said indignantly. "Owen Swann's one of the finest hyperspace navigators in the United West merchant fleet. And I couldn't ask for a better captain than Cat Biko."

"That's a top school, isn't it?" she said to make amends as they entered the lounge.

"Yeah. It's great. They don't turn out morons who can only fly ships. The school's heavy on science, but I take lit. courses, too, and the odd art course when I can squeeze it in."

She'd obviously hit on one of his favorite topics. "It sounds interesting. So what's this internship about?"

"I'm learning hyperspace navigation," he answered, "and I take some real-space navigation from Mizzer Nast too. Then I help out, when I'm not studying. It's not bad, and it pays well. The money will get me through next semester."

Mz Sigmund looked into the lounge. When she saw Puck, she came right over.

"May I have a word?" she asked, and Michael backed off.

"I kind of overreacted last night," Mz Sigmund said, and Puck was disappointed until she heard the woman's next words. "But I did hear those noises. Come tell me if you hear them again. I'd like to get to the bottom of this."

"Sure, Mz Sigmund," Puck said cheerfully. The woman really was nosy, but so was she.

"Call me Leesa," the young woman said, smiling back. "I'll let you get back to your friend. Loki's waiting for me in the dining room."

My friend, Puck thought, pleased. She allowed herself to relax a bit. Maybe Cubuk wouldn't put two and two together.

"So, what's this hyperspace navigator like, then?" Puck asked Michael.

"Oh, he keeps to himself most times. He's very private. Hyperspace navigators are like that. It's probably the stress," he said, nodding seriously. Then his face lit up. "But you should see his jumps. He can make numbers dance to music, so you can see unknown geometry. It takes a cosmic wizard to juggle the formulae at a moment's notice, bounce around what's out there and get a ship out again at exactly the right place. But it's not only mathematics; you have to feel it in your bones."

"And do you feel it?" Puck asked, fascinated.

He turned away, pushing a handful of thick black hair from his forehead. "I don't know for sure yet," he muttered. "Owen hardly ever lets me try."

"But you want to real bad," she said.

He laughed that short bark of amusement that she was coming to identify with him. "Well, I've got to specialize in something. I'm not sure I want to end up like Owen, though."

"What do you mean?"

"He talks to himself all the time. Not just when he talks himself through jumps, but in the corridors and at meals —when he actually eats with us. People think his brain is a bit space-warped. Of course they say that you have to be crazy to begin with to see through hyperspace, and if you don't start that way, you soon will be." He looked so solemn for a moment that Puck realized he was really worried about it.

"Well, you're going to be a good one, then," she said, poking him to get his mind off it.

"Hey," he cried, jumping back.

"But right now you're only a glorified cabin boy," she continued, advancing on him, finger ready.

He fended her off playfully as he backed up, and almost collided with the ladies as they entered the lounge.

Mz Dante frowned, but Mz Florette had a soppy, lop-sided smile on her face. "Hello, hearts," she said.

Puck's hands went automatically behind her back. "Hi," she said, feeling foolish. She noticed Michael looked uncomfortable too. Luckily the ladies didn't stop to coo and embarrass them further. Mz Florette's perfume receded as they swept away.

"One more left now," said Michael.

God, not Cubuk, she thought.

"So tell me, what are you doing?" Michael asked.

"I'm a student of life," she tossed off, trying to seem casual. It sounded stupid as soon as she'd said it.

Michael's lips curved wryly. "Student of sixth grade is more like it."

"Seventh," she shot back angrily.

"I meant what's on Aurora for you?"

Puck could tell he was amused. "I'm going to join my parents. They're doing important research for the government." The words came out snottier than she'd intended. She tried to lighten up. "I haven't seen them in ages. It's going to be absolute zero." A familiar tightness crept into her stomach.

"Are they helping the Shoowa develop that one-man hyperskip?" he asked.

"No," she answered, wondering what that was all about. "They're xenobiologists. They study alien life."

Michael gestured toward the door. "Speaking of alien life . . ."

The alien stood there, peering anxiously around him as if unsure that this was where he should be.

"Good day," Michael called to him. "This way for the tour."

Puck was delighted. Cubuk wasn't coming, the alien was. Here was her chance to make friends with him.

The alien's neck bulged as if he gulped with fear, but his gait as he walked toward them had a strange double bounce in it that hinted of joy at being invited in such a friendly way.

Puck looked curiously at the pendant he wore, the one he'd held to the corridor wall. Part of it seemed to be there yet not there. It made her go cross-eyed when she tried to look at it. Was this the alien version of pretty?

She had finally worked up enough nerve to step forward to greet him, when the croak of a voice made her start.

"That creature is not coming along, is it?"

CHAPTER
FIVE

"For goodness' sake, Beat," said Mz Dante. "He's a guest among us. Be more charitable."

Mz Florette sniffed loudly. "Oh, well. I suppose so. I was not expecting to have to mix with him, that is all."

The alien stared down at his hands, and Puck felt awful for him. Mz Florette bent to retrieve her purse, and Puck poked her tongue out at the woman. She turned to say something to Michael and found the alien looking at her with interest.

"Mz Goodfellow," Michael said, "I believe you already know Mz Dante and Mz Florette." The ladies inclined their heads, almost in unison. "May I present to everyone . . ." Michael hesitated. "Hush Wa Shoon Ya Shan Ya Ha." He stumbled over the name awkwardly.

The alien meshed his long fingers together and held his arms in front of him, head slightly bowed in greeting. The gesture pulled his sleeves back far enough to reveal wrists as knobby as his finger joints.

"Glad to have you along," Mz Dante said crisply.

Mz Florette managed a tight little smile.

Puck copied the alien's gesture, smiling at him encouragingly. He seemed immensely pleased, his face crinkling into even more gray wrinkles. His throat vibrated gently.

She almost squeaked with excitement when he crowned her fists briefly with his own. His hands were warm and dry.

"Let's head for the lift, then," Michael said, and the ladies followed him to the door.

The alien waited expectantly for Puck, so she fell in beside him. She was surprised when he raised a finger for her attention. Deliberately he turned his head in the direction of Mz Florette's back, his neck seemed to elongate an inch or so, and slowly a tongue emerged from his mouth. It was purple.

He looked at Puck, and his throat expanded and contracted as it had when he came into the room. That was laughter, she realized. They had shared a joke. Maybe it wouldn't be hard to make friends with him after all. She ran ahead of him, chuckling—to find Cubuk waiting outside, the others gone.

Cubuk took a step toward her. He looked angry. Then the alien came out of the door behind her, and Cubuk turned on his heel and walked away.

"Come on," Puck said to the alien, her voice trembling. "Let's catch up." She hurried down the corridor and rejoined Michael and the ladies outside the passenger lift.

"What's that?" she asked Michael loudly, pointing to a door marked with a stick figure by the passenger lift. If Cubuk was still near, she wanted him to know she was part of a group, that she wasn't going to be alone.

"Emergency stairs," Michael answered. "In case the lifts

break down. They're kept locked." He called the lift. "*Cat's Cradle* hires out as a tramp freighter," he said to the group.

But Puck couldn't concentrate on his explanation. And what made it worse was to be next to Mz Florette, who was wearing a perfume that Puck was sure had been invented to repel children. The woman also breathed loudly through her mouth. Probably so she wouldn't have to smell herself, Puck decided.

They stepped out of the lift into a pocket in the center of the bridge and had to walk up a short flight of stairs to deck level. The large core was left behind, and the slim tower that protruded through the floor held only enough space for the passenger lift.

The room they were in covered the entire deck. Unintelligible lights and dials were everywhere, along with strategically positioned chairs and padded flight couches.

Above was a huge dome. It took her breath away. Black as the velvet of eternity, it was splattered with stars. If not for the faintly luminous lines that bisected this cupola of night, she would have thought the tip of the ship sliced off, and felt herself topple out into the universe.

"You'll get a crick in your neck," a rich, friendly voice said, and Puck tore her eyes away. Captain Biko advanced cheerfully to greet her passengers. "Welcome to the bridge."

"Hi, Captain Cat," Puck said. She pointed up. "Is that real?"

Captain Biko laughed. "That's exactly what most people

wonder on their first trip up here, but it usually takes them longer to ask. It's a simulation of what is actually occurring outside at this moment—a real-time projection from outside sensors. Not only does it make us believe we are actually going somewhere more convincingly than all the instruments in the galaxy, but it certainly helps my claustrophobia."

"It's gorgeous," Puck said, and the captain glowed with pride as if she had invented it.

"Then you'll also be fascinated by another one of our navigational aides. . . ."

Captain Biko gave them a full tour, and Puck had to admit that some of the explanations—no, many of them—went in one ear and out the other. How did anyone keep all these flashing lights and readouts straight? Did Michael really understand all this? She found her admiration for him growing. *I wish I could be a captain,* she thought. But you had to be good in school to do something like that.

It was hard to tell what the alien thought of the tour, and Mz Dante nodded politely, but Puck didn't think much was sinking in. Mz Florette, however, swiveled her head this way and that, bright-eyed like a greedy little bird. She didn't ask questions, but every so often she let out interested clicks and hums.

Michael followed the tour with the rest of them, but had eyes only for Captain Biko. Hmmm. Did he have a crush on his captain? Puck wondered, feeling a pang of jealousy.

"And this is the place where our jumps are coordinated," the captain said. "The nerve center for hyperspace navigation."

They were in front of a raised dais that held a heavily padded chair fronted by a wall of instruments that gently curved toward the seat. The arms of the chair were studded with controls.

"The hyperspace navigator negotiates the jumps from here," the captain explained. "It's a delicate operation that requires vast skill and intense concentration. During the jumps a force field is generated to protect the navigator from distraction." She pointed to what Puck had thought were lamps embedded in the rim of the dais.

"And some say, to protect us from the navigator," Michael muttered.

"We usually leave it on to guard the delicate instruments when we're not in jump," the captain said. "The hyperspace navigator holds the only key. It's become a tradition. Of course he'd better keep the key on his person at all times, else I'll have his skin." She chuckled, softening the threat.

"Where does he see hyperspace?" Puck asked Michael quietly.

"Up there." He pointed at the dome.

Puck looked up again. "That means anyone here could see." Maybe she'd get a chance.

"Look," Michael said. "But not always see. It's a special skill. I mean, all most people see is an uncomfortable blur that makes them want to throw up. Scientists don't know why—they're still studying it—but not everyone can look into hyperspace."

"But you can."

"Yeah," he said, sounding smug. "That's what makes hyperspace navigators special."

"Maybe it's a brain defect," she said, and he narrowed his eyes. She smiled wickedly. "So, it must be pretty messy up here during jumps with everyone whoopsing all over the place."

Michael couldn't help laughing at the disgusting image. "Nah. There's only a couple of technicians around then to keep things going, and the captain, but she won't look up."

"Captain Cat throws up?" Puck felt a little disappointed.

A side door opened abruptly, and a slim man with flyaway, mousy hair hurried by them to the navigator's chair. His arms were loaded down with a quartet of black, shiny boxes, each about twenty centimeters square.

All the way there he slapped at something invisible, as if it blocked his way, and his load slid precariously to one side before he caught it. "All around," he muttered. "Wish they'd leave me alone."

"That's our hyperspace navigator," Michael said, "Owen Swann."

Puck stared after him. "Oh, I feel really safe now."

The captain spotted the navigator too. "Owen, there you are. I'd like you to meet our guests."

He swiveled toward her to say something, but he never got it out. His face went white, and the pile of boxes tumbled to the floor.

"Oh, no!" he gasped.

CHAPTER
SIX

The captain sighed. "Pick up those cubes, Owen."

But Owen Swann either ignored her or didn't hear. He was staring at the alien.

The alien's gray face gradually creased into wrinkles, which Puck took to be an expression of puzzlement. He bowed his lanky form slightly in Swann's direction and spoke. "At your service, Mizzer." His voice glugged like water poured from a full-bellied pitcher. Puck was thrilled.

Swann's hand flew to his mouth. "Y-You're real, are you?" he managed to stammer out.

"I exist," the alien said hesitantly.

Owen Swann's hands skimmed through the air like distracted birds. "But who are the others?"

"Others?" The alien's face became even more wrinkled, if that were possible.

"Never mind. I don't think I want to know." Swann stooped and hurriedly piled his spilled load into a unit he could lift. "I've got to think about this," he said to himself, and turned back to the door.

"When you have," said Captain Biko sternly, "please come explain to me."

"Yes, yes," he said absently, fumbling with the lock.

He looked so frantic, Puck couldn't stand it. She rushed

over and slapped the release plate for him. He gave her a brief, surprised smile and slid through while the door was still opening. Puck caught a glimpse of a small office filled mostly by a table piled high with more of those bizarre boxes.

"I never thought Owen was a xenophobe," Michael whispered when Puck rejoined him.

"I'm afraid hyperspace navigators can be a little eccentric," the captain said to the alien. "I hope you won't take offense."

The alien bowed slightly accepting her apology.

"I believe this portion of your tour is over, Mizzer Tse."

"Yes, Mz." Michael dutifully herded his group into the lift.

The alien stood beside the perfumed Mz Florette. He looked down at her sideways, his flat nostrils twitching. She was trying to edge away from him. Cocking her head, Puck caught his eye and winked in wicked sympathy, then she carefully raised her fingers to pinch her nose without the old lady seeing. The alien glanced down quickly, his throat vibrating. She'd made him laugh again.

"I'm only going to stop for a peek at the next floor down," Michael said as the lift came to a halt with a hiss. "This is the captain's and officers' quarters."

The lift opened to reveal a corridor like that on the guest level. Mizzer Ernest stood outside a cabin. He whirled to face them, slapping the plate of his door as he did. "Don't you announce your tours, Mizzer?" he snapped.

Puck thought she saw a leg in some kind of padded covering disappear as the cabin door closed.

"I left a message on the work screens," Michael said, looking surprised.

The second mate appeared to collect himself. "Yes, yes, you must have. I hadn't noticed, I'm afraid." He seemed abashed at his outburst. "You startled me."

"Sorry, Mizzer Ernest. Just having a quick look," Michael replied, and closed the lift door. He rolled his eyes heavenward for her benefit, and Puck realized that Michael thought Mizzer Ernest a bit of a fool.

"Is that where your cabin is?" she asked.

"No, thank goodness," Michael answered. "I'm down in Engineering. It's a bit more casual down there."

"We'll skip the lounge deck, loading bay, and guest deck," he continued, taking on an official tone again as he addressed the whole group. "I thought I'd show you the lower freight deck as an example of our storage areas."

They stepped out into a large open space. Little cosmetic covering was used here; the ribs and joints of the inner shell clearly showed. The bigger ribs that emerged from the walls were bulkheads that defined large, open bays loaded with crates. The crates were slotted carefully together like a child's blocks and were secured by a glittering metallic mesh attached to the ribs. The back crates fit neatly, diamond fashion, into notches in the hull.

"*Cat's Cradle* is a container ship," Michael said. "We provide the containers; whoever contracts us fills them. We have different sizes. . . ." Michael droned on, and Puck lost interest.

The alien's hands were agitated as if they could find no comfortable place to be. Puck didn't know why he was upset. Maybe if she did something friendly, he'd feel better.

She remembered the chocolate in her pocket. But did he eat Earth food? Well, just offering was good enough, wasn't it? She took out the bar, snapped off a chunk, and held it up to him. He looked down at the candy, then at her, not sure of what to do. She popped it into her mouth and made a big show of enjoying it, then she held out another piece. He took the chocolate gingerly and carefully placed it into his mouth. His eyes grew big, and his narrow lips pinched together. *Oh, God. I've killed him,* Puck thought. But his eyes closed, and his purple tongue snaked out to lick his lips. His throat glugged fast in pleasure. "A taste wonderful," he said. "My thanks."

He likes chocolate, Puck thought triumphantly. *He's a real person.*

"The freight elevator runs all the way from the upper freight deck, where the loading bay is, down to Engineering," Michael was saying. "On the engineering deck and the freight decks the lift opens on either side to make loading and unloading easier."

The alien touched something on one of the bulkheads—a raised design that had been painted over—and the lines on his face all seemed to travel downward, giving him a worried expression. His throat looked deflated and wattled like an old man's. That was the opposite of laughter, she guessed.

He looked down at her with dark, unreadable eyes. "They have done an excellent job," he said.

"What job?" she asked.

"The conversion."

A horrible sound from Mz Florette cut off Puck's next question. "Yikk! What is it?"

Puck turned to see Mz Florette clutching her voluminous gauzy culottes close to her legs. The slight paralysis of her face had became more pronounced, so that her words were slurred. "It rubbed my ankle! Shtop it."

"It" sat at Michael's feet—a small black-and-white cat, imperiously inspecting Mz Florette as if she were a lunatic.

"It's only a cat," Mz Dante said, emphasizing the last two words.

"Of coursh it ish," Mz Florette answered hastily, but she didn't loosen the grip on her pants. "I hate them. They are shlinky, and furry, and they run up your legsh."

Puck choked back a laugh. "No, they don't."

"There's your noise last night," Mz Dante said to her companion. "It was a cat howling."

So they'd heard it, too, Puck thought, as she crouched on the floor and wiggled her fingers invitingly. "Here, puss." The cat sauntered obligingly toward her.

"Podkayne's a friendly little cat," Michael said. "She

wouldn't hurt anyone. You should see her son, Harriman, though. He's a wacking great orange tomcat. I wouldn't bet on the rat."

Puck stroked the velvety head. "Come on. There's no rats on this ship."

Michael grinned. "See, it works."

Puck threatened him playfully with her fist.

"Every ship needs working cats, that's what the captain says. The other Earthside captains think she's nuts, but she likes the nickname they gave her."

"Cat," Puck said. "And the ship's called *Cat's Cradle* for more than one reason." She was pleased by the joke.

"Yeah, it's a good excuse to have pets aboard."

"Pets?" the alien asked.

"An animal friend," Puck answered, excited that he was talking to her now. "Have you had one?"

"No," he answered. "That is a thing of stories; a warm thing my people have not in a long time had." He watched her stroke the cat. "Would it let me?" He folded into a crouch beside her, his robe expanding tentlike, and carefully reached out a hand.

Puck waited with delighted expectation.

Softly he gave the cat's back one stroke with the tips of his fingers, and Podkayne let out an encouraging *myap*.

He snatched his hand back. "What does it say?"

Puck laughed, but answered gently. "I don't know; we can't speak to them. Listen, though, you can hear her purr." She smoothed the dark fur until Podkayne rumbled. "It's like your throat." She touched her own throat so that he would understand, and hoped he wouldn't be offended.

"Ohwo," he said. The information appeared to satisfy him immensely, for his throat began to pulsate with the purr, and he reached out to touch the cat again.

"Well, I think animals should be chained up," came Mz Florette's panicky falsetto. To emphasize her point, she gestured toward an unusually intricate chain that was strung across the mouth of a bay. It was too absurdly large to hold a cat.

A strangled sound made Puck turn back to the alien. As he stared at the chain, the color drained from his face. All eyes were on him as he crashed to the floor.

CHAPTER
SEVEN

"Can't you give him something?" Puck asked Mizzer Ernest once they got to sick bay.

"Just give him some room to breathe and let him come round by himself," Mizzer Ernest said, tugging at his jacket neck nervously. "Anything I give him could do more harm than good."

The captain arrived and dismissed the two crew members who had carried the alien up. Michael ushered the ladies along to the mess hall with promises of a lovely lunch.

Mizzer Ernest cleared his throat. "Well, I'm off. I'll send a tech down to watch him."

Puck snorted. "He didn't do anything."

"He can't help that," the captain said, drawing Puck toward the door. "We really don't know enough. It'll change fast now, with all the experts studying our new friends."

Puck nodded. "That's what my parents are doing on Aurora," she said. "They're part of the xeno-team."

"Good for them," said Captain Biko. "That takes skill and dedication."

Puck felt a warm glow of pride. Most people hadn't a clue. Planet exploration to them was all the zip-zip of lasers in a cheap vid, and wrestling tentacled monsters, not late nights in an ill-equipped lab, light-years from home. But skill and dedication were hard to live up to.

"Hey, get some lunch with the others," the captain said. "Okay?"

"I'm not hungry. Can I stay?" Puck asked. "He needs a friend, remember?"

Captain Biko rested a hand briefly on Puck's shoulder. "Yes, I think that's a good idea. I'll tell Mizzer Ernest. Use that com if you need help."

After the captain left, Puck had a moment's panic. What if Cubuk found her here? But no, he'd backed off last time when he'd seen her with the alien. She was safe for now.

She sat on the end of the sick-bay couch and waited anxiously for signs of recovery. *Poor guy,* she thought. *It must be scary to be ill with no one like you near, and no one knowing how to help.* She remembered her first week at boarding school, when she missed Gran desperately and cried every night, until her scuzzy roommate heard her and told everyone. For weeks girls screeched, "Boo-hoo-hoo," when they passed her in the hallway. *Really made me feel at home,* she thought bitterly, and thumped her fist into the couch.

The alien turned his head to her and opened his large, dark eyes.

"Whoops," she said. "Did I disturb you?"

He shook his head. "That means no, yes?" he asked.

She smiled before she could think about it. "Yes."

He sat up slowly and his feet found the floor. She was

fascinated to see him reach back and scratch himself easily in a place no human could have touched. He seemed to be getting his normal color back, his skin returning from an ashy pale to a deeper gray.

"Please," he said, "I am detaining you."

"I don't mind," she answered. "Honest. You all right?"

"Yes," he said, and nodded his head as if trying that gesture for the first time also.

"Can I get you something?" she asked.

"Do you have more of that sweet taste?" he said hopefully.

She laughed, and pulled the candy out of her pocket. "Chocolate."

"Shockalate," he repeated as he took the chunk she offered.

"What happened?" she asked.

He let out a burst of air, like a sigh. "I saw a something that made a bad thing worse, and it frightened me."

His hands covered his mouth for a moment as if refusing to let the words out, but he continued. "I tried not to believe at first, but the making of that chain in the hold made everything truth. I am afraid because this is being a Grakk ship."

"It's not," Puck cried.

"It is," he insisted. "There are Grakki symbols everywhere." He pointed to a raised pattern on the wall like the one he'd stared at in the hold. "It is to picture a nova," he said. "The Grakk make worship to it as the sun god who drove them out to conquer all worlds."

"Wow," Puck said. She knew that some of the Grakk vessels impounded during the war had been sold off by the government, but she'd never suspected that this was one of them. But why should that be such a surprise? she thought. Humans had been using Grakk technology ever since Santiago's Mistake, when the first Grakk ship had been accidentally captured and humans solved the mystery of hyperdrive.

"It is a cruel joke to be going home on a Grakk ship," the alien said. "A same ship that took my people to be slaves. It is like a punishment for what I have done."

"But what have you done?" Puck asked.

"Please, I cannot talk about this more," he said.

Puck didn't want to push, so she changed the subject. "What's your name, again? I mean, I know I heard, but it's kinda long."

"Hushwa'shoonyashanyaha." It came out in a liquid rush, nowhere near the way Michael had said it. Then the alien raised his right hand, held the two thumbs together, and touched the first of his three fingers to his flat nose.

"Absolute zero," Puck said. "Say it again."

He repeated the name, and once again touched his nose.

"Got an itch?" she asked, pointing to her nose.

"It's my name end." He sounded surprised that she hadn't understood.

"What, touching your nose?" Michael hadn't realized it, either, she thought smugly; he'd left that part out. "I like your name," she said. "It sort of whooshes."

"*Hush* is the sound of the wind in the northern mountains of my people's home," he said, "but I have never heard it. My birth-parent's birth-parent knew it from her childhood and named me from remembrance."

"Your grandmother named you," Puck guessed.

"Yes. My birth-parent died of the sorrow of giving a child to slavery. My grandmother had much in the say of my raising."

"Yeah, I know what that can be like," Puck said. Who would have thought they had something like that in common?

"It was also the name of my grandmother's womb mate, her dead brother," the alien explained. "He was a person well loved. She said I would one day carry the name home to our planet again."

"To Aurora," Puck said.

"To Shoon," the alien answered, using his people's word.

"Hey, that's part of your name." Puck was delighted. "Your name's got a meaning?"

He nodded.

"Okay." She giggled. "What's this bit?" She touched her nose.

He answered solemnly. "I have not yet smelled my mate."

Puck whooped with laughter before she could help it. "I'm sorry," she gasped finally, "but it sounds so funny."

"I am glad to bring you laughing," he said.

"Maybe that's why Mz Florette wears so much perfume," Puck said. "She's hoping her mate will smell her."

"I believe the female is being too old for childbearing," the alien answered, and Puck would have thought he'd missed the joke, except she saw the vibration in his throat. "You gave me much humor in the lift today," he said. Puck remembered touching her nose and burst out laughing again. She'd made a pun and hadn't known.

"Are you old enough to be married?" she asked.

"It would be allowed," he answered. "But I would be young for this. I must find my life first."

Settle on what he should be doing, like a job, she supposed. That made him a grown-up, but he hadn't been one for long.

"Perhaps I will never have the finding of a mate," he said. "I am not beautiful."

Gosh, who could tell? Puck thought. "Is there a sign for married men?" she asked.

He put his finger to his lips. "I have tasted joy."

That made her feel warm somehow.

"So your name means . . ."

" 'Hush of the Asha people of Northern Shoon, unmated son,' " he finished for her.

"Can I just call you Hush?"

"That is better than Yikkth, which is what the Grakk

called me. It means 'water contaminated with indigestible microorganisms.'" He looked mournful, but his throat glugged.

Pond scum, she realized, and joined in his laughter again.

I can't believe it, we're joking together like old friends, she thought. *That's what I'd planned,* she remembered, and felt a bit guilty.

"You are kind, Mz Goodfellow," Hush said.

"My friends call me Puck."

He held his palm out. "Has it a meaning?"

She shrugged her shoulders. "I was a small, pink baby, like an elf, Mom said. Robin Goodfellow—Puck—they're both names for a tiny person in a story, who lives in the woods and causes trouble. It probably serves my parents right if I act like a troublemaker." She thought of the head-mztress frowning down on her and of her cases neatly stacked by the school's main door.

"A story name," Hush said. "My people do this too. I know of a person named after a hero who married a great queen—but this person died young and never found his mate. We do not always become our names."

"Guess not," she said, unconvinced.

He sat in silence staring at his spidery hands. Then he reached out to touch her softly on the arm, and his strange eyes caught hers. "I have made shameful my name," he said. "It will never be given to another young one."

"But why?" she asked, shocked.

"I have lost a thing entrusted to me. Something of my

people's heart and history, that now might never be brought home."

She should have felt excitement at making him talk, but she could only feel his loss.

CHAPTER
EIGHT

"What happened?" Puck asked.

Hush sighed and raised his long hands helplessly.

"Start at the very beginning," Puck said, like Gran would have.

"Oh Kay." Hush folded his hands in his lap. "It is being twelve of your years since the end of the war, and my people are still on Grubblikk, the planet of their captivity." He clicked his *k*s like a Grakk.

"Many ships were built on Grubblikk, and messages came from all places Grakk were. Much work was there for slaves who could learn languages and had clever fingers. We became of much knowledge.

"When your people came, Earth had many questions about the machines the Grakk made. Who might they learn better these things from, the conquered enemy or the grateful captive freed?"

"They could have tortured the Grakk with water drips," Puck said half seriously. Grakk skin had a horrendous reaction to water. The few Grakk prisoners of war were imprisoned on a moon where it rained all the time, so they didn't dare escape.

"Grakk are with luck that your adults are not so fierce," Hush said, but his throat glugged with amusement.

"My people traveled with the Grakk for many years. Four of your lifetimes, I am thinking. We could find the places they had been; we could read the Grakki writings; we could speak to the races Earth didn't know, and help find the homes of the other slave peoples. Earth had uses for us.

"We worked hard to prove ourselves friends and hurry our own way home. But long years of war make people doubt. The questions humans asked made us realize they did not trust. If they sent us home, would we be another enemy to fight?" He bowed his head.

"There were many waitings. And then they talked of money. Who would be paying for us to go home?" He shook his domed head in dismay. "It seems a strange that kindness is not more important. We were still to do the work of another race. We still were not free."

Puck felt embarrassed for mankind. *Are we as bad as the Grakk?* she wondered. Her parents were on Shoon already, before all the people who truly deserved to go, and she was on the way there too.

"But we did not find fear of humans," Hush explained. "They were not cruel, just greedy for knowledge and not stopping to think of others' pain. We became bold. Did Earth want us to become silent and stupid with sorrow? we asked.

"Many people had many meetings, and finally agreement was made. Some Shoowa would stay on Grubblikk, and some would travel with Earth people. In return others could go home to Shoon.

"One had to come at the front to make plans with the home world. This one was me. I would bring home hope that kin lived out in the stars; but, most important, I was to bring home the symbol of our freedom, the Soowa'asha—Child of the Asha."

He tensed and clenched the same fist she had secretly seen him pound on his thigh yesterday.

"I am the last in the family of its protectors. My grandmother put it into my arms. They all had trust in me."

"What is it?" Puck asked.

"The Soowa'asha is a thing of our distant past," he said. "Long ago, on Shoon, before I had birth or my grandmother had birth, nations fought each other. The Asha were thrown to the ground by a people from the south, the Zhigh. The . . ." He paused as if seeking the word. "The king of the Zhigh, to show his much power over us, said we were not worthy to have children. An Asha child would be taken and raised as Zhigh, to increase the Zhigh nation.

"At first my people had no believing, but then three new-births were taken, and amid the cries of the sorrowing birth-parents a vow was made. The Asha would not again be seen to have children until they were free. Children would mean freedom, and freedom was a child.

"The artist Rushuwa'danya made a statue shaped to the form of freedom, the size of a newborn young. This will be our child, the old wise ones said, until we can have children of the flesh. And they set it up in a beautiful house of woven sweet grass so that the people from all villages could have the seeing of it and be firm in their vow."

Puck wondered how you could make the shape of freedom, but she didn't interrupt.

"The Zhigh made laughter at us," Hush continued. "Mate will call to mate, they said, and children will be born despite your foolish statue. But the old grew older and died. The young people had no mating dances. There were no life-mates bound with the flowers of blessing. And females sickened and took to their beds with the longing for children—or so the Zhigh thought. But, in the truth, it was with the birthing of secret children. It was the Zhigh who were foolish ones.

"Children were smuggled out to the hills, to our friends, the people of the caves. They raised our children to sing one song, and half a lifetime later a multitude of children charged from the hills, the peoples they had befriended in their travels rushed in from the sea, and the aging birth-parents had the last laughter at the fleeing backs of the Zhigh."

Puck could almost see the triumphant battle. "Wow," she said. "That would make a great vid. So then what happened to the statue?"

"The Soo was kept as a remember of our freedom and victory. People walked from many places to see it. They said if a female who could bear no young touched it, she would flower in birth. New children were dedicated to the power of life in its presence.

"When the Grakk came, the keeper of the Soo hid it under his clothings so it would not be made dirty by their hands. But he was taken aboard their ship before he could make it safeness, and it went into slavery with us.

"The Soo was made hidden all those years, and whispered in our hearts that one day we would have free. Many times it had danger, and Shoowa gave their lives to keep it from the Grakk. I was to have the bringing of the Soo home; instead I had the losing of it." His face looked taut and harsh, as it had before he'd fainted.

He stood up suddenly in a multijointed flow, and she felt the weight of his tight misery constrict her heart. "I have failed my people. I am worse than Grakk feces." He walked away.

"No," she said, following him. "I know it's not your fault. Tell me what happened."

He looked back as she took his arm gently and felt the strange lumps of his alien architecture beneath her fingers.

"I am honored by your trust," he said, and his features that had become stony softened again. "Now I need some aloneness. Later I will tell you—after the sundown meal perhaps."

"Promise?" Puck asked.

He bobbed his head yes.

Puck watched him leave. "Scuzz," she mumbled. She hoped he'd feel better later.

She wandered into the lounge and found the Sigmunds chuckling over an old horror threedee. Puck wondered what was so amusing. She dropped into a nearby chair and hooked into the sound. There was a lot of screaming and a chase through some woods at night, then the scene shifted to inside a gloomy old castle. A gruesome creature was wavering and distorting. It was changing shape, changing into a woman.

Good God! thought Puck. *That's Mz Dante!*

CHAPTER
NINE

"You mean you didn't know that Antonia Dante was an old vid star?" Loki Sigmund said.

"No," Puck answered gleefully. "I watch a lot of old vids too. You'd think I would have recognized her."

"Well, maybe not," Mizzer Sigmund said. "She was well known for her monster roles. She was one of the makeup experts of her day."

"Yeah," joined in Leesa Sigmund. "They used to say, 'Don't step on it, it might be Antonia Dante.'"

Puck laughed. She wondered if Mz Dante would tell her all about those days. "It must be a comedown for her to be riding on this ship when she's probably used to luxury liners," she said, then blushed because, of course, the Sigmunds might feel the same way.

"I don't think they were registered on the *Star Queen* in the first place," Mizzer Sigmund said. "The purser let me look at the passenger list to see if there was someone we could go in with on a private yacht."

"I heard she gambles." Leesa whispered the words with relish.

"Now, where did you hear that?" her husband asked, impatient with the gossip.

"In a magazine," Leesa replied indignantly. "She squandered away all the money she made, and that's why she's still entertaining the troops on every outpost even though the war's been over for years."

So maybe she wouldn't want to talk about her vid career after all, Puck thought. Pity.

Her stomach chose that moment to rumble, and she remembered the lunch she'd missed. "I'm going to find a snack," she said. "Thanks for letting me watch with you."

She managed to scrounge a sandwich from the little guy who worked in the galley—although he wasn't particularly friendly—then she went back to her room.

—

Puck was leaving for dinner when she heard a noise in the direction of the freight lift—a scrabbling sound like nails on metal. She caught her breath, remembering the sounds of the night before. *This is a fully lit corridor and it's not night,* she told herself. But night was a planet-bound distinction, wasn't it? Maybe in space it was always night.

She could ignore the noise and head the other way to the passenger lift, but despite her thumping heart, curiosity lured her on.

All the doors were shut tight, and she could see nothing on the metal walls or the endless hexagonal pattern of the carpet. The only thing that stirred was the occasional gust of warm air on her ankles from the floor-level circulation vents. But the scrabbling sound continued, like something trapped trying to escape.

A moan erupted near her feet, freezing her in shock. "Oooowahhhhhhhhhhhhhrghhh!"

A nearby grate shifted and jerked.

A pale blob oozed from under it.

"Purrrrp!" the blob said. A large ginger tomcat stood blinking at her.

Puck exploded into a gasping laugh. "You gave me quite a scare," she said as the cat wound itself around her legs. "You must be Harriman. Ooof! You'll knock me over."

So to save him the trouble, and to rest her trembling legs, she sat on the floor to make friends.

She'd been quietly petting the cat for only a few minutes when the door to the cabin opposite the freight lift opened slightly and she heard voices.

"Come on, Cubuk, let me in on it." That was Mz Sigmund.

"Forget it. I'm just on vacation," Cubuk growled.

"Oh, come on," insisted Mz Sigmund. "Wherever you are, there's bound to be alien treasure. What are you after?"

"Look. I'm not after anything, and if you tell any stories about me to anyone, I'll make you regret it. You're pushing it, girl. A few words to the right people and you're finished. Understand me?"

"You wouldn't." Mz Sigmund's voice was trembling now.

"Wouldn't I?" His laugh was cruel.

Oh, my God, he'd have her killed, thought Puck. *I can't be here when they come out.* She scrambled to her feet and ran back the way she had come.

—

"That's how the cats get around," Michael said at dinner. "Through the repair tunnels and crawl spaces between decks. We close off the places that might be dangerous, but they've got the run otherwise."

The ladies sat with the captain and Mizzer Cubuk at the next table. It made Puck's flesh crawl to have Cubuk so close. He whispered in the captain's ear, and she laughed with delight. Every so often she put her hand on his and let it linger there. He acted like an ordinary, charming dinner companion, instead of a vicious criminal. But Puck knew better.

"Would you like some water?" Cubuk asked Mz Florette, who was smothering her roast chicken with salt.

"Oh, no, no, no," she replied, waving the proffered jug away, and devoured another mouthful.

"Do you know anything about him?" Puck said.

Michael shrugged. "Owen said they met on the captain's last shore leave." He didn't seem pleased.

Puck was happy that the captain hadn't known Cubuk long. Maybe she didn't know about his other life. Perhaps Puck should say something. But how do you tell a woman you hardly know that the man she likes might be a killer?

Leesa Sigmund was watching the captain and Cubuk too. She didn't look scared. That surprised Puck. Was she too interested in what he was after to let him bother her? Alien treasure, she'd said. That must have been what she was looking for last night.

Puck glanced over at the table where Hush ate his vegetables alone. She had invited him to sit with them when he'd appeared at the door, but "I'm not usual to eating with humans," he'd said. "I might not be liking the food. I do not want to be watched not liking it."

Yeah, she thought. *I can grab that.* She hoped he hadn't changed his mind about telling her more this evening. Maybe she had something to tell him.

Michael stood up to take his plate to the garbage disintegrator. "Gonna go zap my leftovers and hit the study holos," he said. "The other passengers are planning to watch a vid in the lounge. Going?"

"Nah," Puck answered. "I already saw one this afternoon. Anyway, I've got a date."

"What? Who with? The man in the moon?" Michael said, chuckling.

"Sort of," she muttered to herself. He really did think of her as just a kid. But she didn't have time to dwell on her pique, because a shadow fell over the end of the table.

"I would like to talk now," Hush said.

CHAPTER
TEN

Puck's couch held Hush like a padded throne, and Puck sat on the floor amid a tumble of cushions as she listened to his tale.

"Things were not being so bad," he said, "until the transfer on Chiron. A female led me to a long line of people, and left me. I could feel the people whisper about me. Stones lay heavy in my stomachs.

" 'Your bags,' a young male said at me. 'What do you have?'

"I laid the pouch that held the Soo to the side so I could put my pack on his desk. He poked at my pack with a skinny finger. Perhaps he thought it a wild beast playing dead. He opened it and moved his hands through quickly, careful of traps and things that bite. His nose flattened, as if my clothes smelled bad. 'What's this?' he said, 'What's this?' "

Puck could tell by the way Hush sat stiffly that he felt again the indignity he must have felt then.

"Then he reached for the Soo pouch," Hush said. " 'No!' I cried. But he swept the pouch to him and opened it. He displayed the Soo to all, like a cheap trinket. 'What's this?' he demanded again. 'Are you having a permit for this?' And he made rough noises about alien plunder.

" 'It is not stolen,' I answered, and tried to take it back, but he held it from me. 'I am taking it home,' I said, reaching for it again, and he held it over his head. 'It is my people's,' I cried.

" 'It may be government property,' he said.

"I was alone. It was an unjust. My unhappy burst, and I howled like a youngling.

"People scattered and the man's mouth opened wide. I grabbed the Soo from his hands. The man cringed and stepped back as if I would hit him, and I howled even louder in my shame. His color changed, and his hands waved. I thought he had pain, but he was breaking a laser alarm, for soon others came running. Men in blue suits, all alike. I had fear for my life.

"I knelt to the floor and bowed my head in give-up, but made safe the Soo to me in my arms, and no one would take it from me. I closed my eyes."

Hush hunched forward, as if he crouched on that floor again. "I heard voices arguing.

"Then there was the *click, click* of officer shoes, and a voice with authority. Everyone said 'sir' many times when they spoke to him. I heard people moving away and muttering. Soon I had the feel of cooler air around me.

"Someone knelt beside me. 'It's okay,' a deep voice said. 'I'm taking you to your ship right now. No more trouble.' And he did."

"So, that wasn't when you lost the Soo," Puck said.

"Not then," Hush responded. "But because of it. If

there had been no fuss, the thief would have had no knowing of the Soo. Of this I am sure."

"But why would anyone take the Soo?" she asked.

Hush's hands wandered in the air, as if feeling for answers. "At first I thought cruelty. But, no. Cruelty is a thing of the moment, not a planned thing. It was greed I am thinking. Yes, greed."

Puck nodded. There'd been many stories in the news vids lately about alien relics disappearing, or turning up on the black market.

"We docked at Earth Station," Hush said, "and this time a human, much kinder, stayed by my side to be helping. I was homed in a tiny cubicle on the space station. There I could sleep while I waited five days for the *Star Queen* to leave."

"It's a pity they don't let aliens down on Earth," Puck said.

"I have sadness for that," he agreed. "I will never be having another chance. But to my much surprise, the station master came to my room. He greeted me friendly and said I could go where I liked to examine and learn. It was fairness, he said, since my people were teaching his so much.

"I spent much time walking, looking, thinking. People stopped me nowhere, but I had sadness; no one called to me as friend. I kept the Soo with me all times, in its pouch belted to my waist. Only one thing made me happiness, to stay at the viewport, looking to the distant spark of home.

"On the third day a short round man with a towel over his arm came to me. 'Excuse me, gentlemizzer,' he said. 'The station master wishes to see you.' And I followed him like a fool."

Hush's last words were stark and angry, his throat swollen and taut. Puck wanted to reach out to him, but was afraid to, so she wrapped her arms tightly around her knees.

"He led me down an empty corridor. His step was light, and I hurried to be keeping up. He looked this way and that way, seeming not sure where to go. *This servant is not usual to this place,* I thought, but I followed still.

"We came to a door. It opened to a room with soft chairs for waiting. 'Please enter,' he said, but did not stand aside to let me easily in. I did not wish to give offend by complaining of his being close, so I squeezed by him, holding my breath against his loud human smell. Somehow we mixed up as I passed. He grabbed to me for balance, tugging my robe. 'Whoops!' he said, and fell. He was on his knees, then up again with much swiftness for his size. I was surprised.

" 'So sorry, so sorry,' he said, patting me with his free hand, urging me into the room. 'Please wait.'

"He left me breathless with his hurry. So muddled that I did not have the notice of the strangeness for a while."

Puck saw the soft wrinkles on Hush's face had stretched into hard lines of anger.

"I waited, and I waited, but no one came. At last I stood,

and then I knew—no weight was banging on my leg. The pouch was slit from cord to seam—the Soo was gone."

He sat silently, his head bowed.

"How long ago was this?" Puck finally asked.

"Two days before the *Star Queen* was to have leaving," Hush answered hesitantly.

Puck had seen the fight the night the *Star Queen* was to have left, and the Soo had already been stolen. "Where is it?" Cubuk had asked. And now Hush and Cubuk were both on the same ship together. It couldn't be an accident. He must have meant the Soo, what else?

"This servant," she asked, "he didn't have hair on his face, did he?"

Hush shook his head. "No. Why do you ask these questions?"

"I just want to understand properly," she answered. "So what did the blue-suits do?"

Hush stared beyond her. "Nothing."

"Nothing?" Puck squeaked.

"I made much noise in the hallways," Hush said. "And there was staring at me in fear. Men in blue suits came and tried to return me to my room. 'I am going to make much noise until someone does something,' I told them, and they took me to a woman behind a big desk. 'Fill out this form, and this form,' she said."

"Just like it was only lost luggage," Puck cried. "Didn't you set her right?"

Hush nodded rapidly. " 'It was stolen,' I said. 'I did not

lose it. That human took it.' Over and over I said this and asked for the station master who had been kindness, so this woman at the desk called someone new.

"I was led to a man in an office, who said the station master was much busy and what was wrong. I said all over again. The man looked angry. 'Why would a human do this?' he asked me. 'If this thing is so important, why were we not told?'

"How could I insult the humans by telling him my people wanted it a secretness, that they did not want to sing a loud song to thieves?

"The man recorded everything, but I had no answers for him that he liked. He said I had confusion from a new place. He said I left it somewheres. I showed him the pouch. 'You tore it,' he said. 'The thing fell out.' It was like beating the clouds.

"At last he sat me at his console and made a picture of the servant with me. 'This is not one of our staff,' he said. 'This is not a real person. Maybe you have the seeing of all humans that way.' I didn't know why he had such angry. I was the one who should have angry.

"He said to search my room, and the other places I had been that day. 'I understand that you wander around,' he said, like that was a bad thing. I felt small.

"I tried to blow up a big wind like my elders might. 'You will be in trouble with your bosses,' I said. 'I was to be traveled safely.' But I have not a voice of power.

" 'I had a brother killed in the war,' he said. He did not

have sense to me. It was not my doing. He waved his hand over a sensor and called in another man."

Hush paused, bundling and unbundling the lap of his robe in his hands. "The man led me to my room. 'Listen,' he said, as if he gave a secret. He told me of many peoples who had no liking of me being there on Earth Station, who said my people were not slaves but partners of the Grakk. Up-top, he said, was thinking me harmless, but people Down-below were thinking it not wise to let me free. He was like a poisonous little shred-beast. I was much glad to reach the safeness of my room.

"I had been holding to hopes of the station master's help, but now I had fear. What if his friendliness was an untruth? It seemed to me then that humans might only be Grakk in different skin."

"I don't think they even told the station master," Puck said. "They preferred you to be miserable because you're an alien. But we're not all like that, honest."

"No. You are not," Hush agreed gently. "But since on that day no one else would help, I would have to be finding it myself."

"How could you know where to start?" Puck asked.

Hush slid from the couch and knelt on the cushions beside her. He held between the thumbs of his right hand the amulet he wore. "With this."

"A necklace?" Puck exclaimed.

He ran a finger through the part you couldn't quite see, producing a gentle hiss. "It is a finder."

"You mean like a homing device?" Puck asked, leaning forward for a better look.

"Yes, that is your words," Hush replied. "There is a transmitter inside the Soo. We stole the workings from the Grakk. It was a safety in the days of slavery, in case the Soo was taken from us. What a strangeness that it not be needed until we are free."

"Why didn't you tell that policeman?" Puck asked.

"Do you think he would have unfolded his ears?"

"No, I guess not," she had to admit.

"So I spent the leftovers of that day and all the next ones searching. I took some sleep when I could barely walk and then began again. But time ran faster than I searched. The next night they would make me leave, and there was one place I had not the look in. I must use the strange freedom the station master gave me, for I was sure that not everyone was allowed out on the docks."

Puck tensed. She knew firsthand what trouble that could get a person into.

"Seven ships sat in dock, their names and destinations on display boards by their berths. Two locks were sealed, ships ready to go. I had the feel of great fear as I walked to these doors. But the Soo was not there. How lucky; one was a private skimmer, it would be much hard to follow; the other, an explorer, would be gone for years.

"A thought made me lighter. Perhaps it was aboard the *Star Queen*. Perhaps I traveled with it.

"I came close with steps of hope. The great lock was

open; workers ran here and there, and hover-loaders carried bags inside. But at the inner door I felt no whisper of the Soo. My hearts fell into dark.

"The next two ships were freighters going to Vega. Their locks lay open, and no one there. But the Soo was not there too.

"There were few ships and few time left. What could I do if I discovered no trail? I almost passed the next open lock, so deep inside worrying I was. But I was grabbed to a stop. My chest rang with the hum of knowing. I took steps into the lock. The feeling grew stronger. The Soo was there. Not thinking to hide, I ran to the inner door. The feel of it close gave me brave. 'Hey, you!' a voice cried. A big man stepped out from inside. 'Get out,' he said. 'This ain't no Hal-oh-een party.'

"I did not stop to make argue, only enough to read the ship's name and the where it was going."

"It was this ship, wasn't it?" Puck said. "And it was going the right way for you to get home too."

"Yes," Hush told her. "*Cat's Cradle* was the only other ship going to my direction, and it had passenger space, the posted stats said."

So, Puck thought, the Soo was already aboard *Cat's Cradle* when Cubuk was trying to beat its whereabouts out of that bearded man on the station. She grinned. "Boy, you lucked out when the *Star Queen* went bust."

Hush's throat responded with equal good humor. "Not so much luck," he said. "The blue-suits wanted me much to leave. If something happened to the liner, they would be putting me on *Cat's Cradle*. Of this I was sure."

"No. You didn't?" Puck squealed. "Did you?" Had this sweet guy sabotaged an entire space liner?

"Finding the way to outside was easy," Hush said. "But the finding of a vacuum suit to fit my longness was not, and the one I chose from the locker room pulled at me most uncomfortable. But it served for the time I needed."

Puck absolutely squirmed with excitement. "You went outside? God, how did you know how?"

"I worked on ships. I have been outside," Hush said. "I loosened some things they would not have the thinking to check. Things hard to find. See."

Hush did something that puzzled her for a moment. He pulled up his sleeve. Then she saw—wrist, elbow, ELBOW, shoulder. No wonder his arms looked long. Wow, the places he could reach.

Puck whooped with laughter. "And that's how you ended up on *Cat's Cradle*. But what now?"

"I keep on searching," he answered. "Because without the Soo I have going home in shame."

"Well, that makes two of us," Puck said.

Hush stared at her. "Why is this?"

"I've been puked."

CHAPTER
ELEVEN

Hush shook his head in confusion. "What is this 'puked'?"

"You know. Thrown up by the system. Expelled. They kicked me out of school." Puck hugged herself defensively.

The way his gray face crumpled made Hush look extremely worried. "Deprive a young one of education? Is this not bad?"

Puck nodded. "My parents are going to be furious. I was supposed to stay in boarding school another year until they were settled."

"But you are still being their child," Hush said. "Will they not have joy seeing you even so?"

Puck sighed. "I don't know. It's a shameful thing, you know."

Hush touched the pouch at his waist. "But you are a gentle, kind young being. Why would they have the doing of this expelling?"

Puck laughed sharply. "No, I'm not. I'm not nice at all. At least I wasn't there. I was really angry at being sent, and the other kids were so snotty. They called me the Yank Midget and stuff. The teachers said dumb things like, 'If you ignore them, they'll stop,' as if that ever worked. I threw a chair across a classroom at one girl. I was always in detention. That's like prison for kids."

Hush raised his hands. "I cannot have the imagine of this." That made Puck feel good.

"But things got better," she said. "Naima Singh started school, and they moved her in with me. She was shy and didn't give me a hard time. Some kids got on her though—'cus of her long, long black hair. They were always coming up behind her and saying, 'Snip, snip, snip.' It was stupid, but the more it bothered her, the more they did it. Her parents would never let her cut her hair; it was important to their religion or something."

Hush nodded. Apparently he understood that.

"She didn't deserve to be tortured, she was a good kid. The next time one of the girls mouthed off to her, I gave the scuzzhead a black eye. Naima and me became best friends after that, even though the head said I was a bad influence.

"Instead of me being a bad influence, I guess Naima was a good one. I can't say I never got into trouble, but not as much, anyway. Some of the other girls even started to be friendly.

"Naima was smart in class, and she was always telling me that I was smart, too, and there was no reason for me to get bad grades. She even offered to help me study, and I tried, I really did. But—I dunno—I could never concentrate on that stuff. It was just so boring."

"And how were you—puked?" Hush asked, his spindly hands folded patiently.

"I failed all my classes for the second quarter in a row,

and I guess I was kinda upset; I set fire to my books in the school yard. Only mine—I didn't burn any that belonged to the school. The head said she might even put up with my bad grades if I at least tried, but I was a troublemaker and she'd had enough. She didn't even understand that I *had* tried."

"I do not find you unwise," Hush said.

Puck bit her lip to hold back tears. "But I must be dumb. And my parents are these superintelligent types, with all these degrees. I'm an embarrassment to them."

Hush stroked her hand. "There are many reasons to not do well in classes. Stupidity is only one."

"Tell that to my parents," Puck said.

"I have sorry for your troubles," Hush said. "It is much hardship for both of us to be facing going home."

"But it's not too late for you," Puck said. "There's still a chance." She felt better to think that at least one of them could land on Aurora with pride. "You can still find the Soo," she said, bouncing to her feet. "I'll help."

Hush crossed his hands, palms out, in front of his chest. "No. I fear that may be danger."

"Why?" Puck protested. Did he know about Cubuk already?

"No," Hush repeated, as she opened her mouth to ask. "I am warmed in my hearts, a child of your people to help a child of mine. But . . ." His hands intertwined, and his agitation stilled her tongue.

"The day I had my leaving," he said, "there was very excitement—blue-suits everywhere."

Puck nodded. "I remember."

"I was answering the boarding call for *Cat's Cradle*, and much eager to be gone, but curious. I picked a hand-com from the belt of a young blue-suit without him knowing, and replayed the message.

"Stuffed in a laundry chute, they had the finding of a man, when the sheets backed up and would not go down. He was several days dead."

Puck gasped before she could help it. She'd been right. It was Bean, the bearded man in the fight with Cubuk. No, Hush said several days dead, it couldn't be Bean.

Hush continued. "He had been hit in the face—a combat attack that sends the nose bone into the brain and kills. He was in his underwears when they had the finding of him. They said he was a valet. That is another word for servant, is it not? A servant like the one who lied to me. A servant who might not have been a servant after all, but a crafty thief."

Puck understood what he meant. Someone had killed the valet and taken his clothes for a disguise. She felt icy cold.

"With this servant being dead," Hush said, "perhaps someone was now on the way to fetch me, to be hearing from me again. Should I delay and demand that they believe me now? I did not think so. I knew where the Soo was. I did not have the time for unkind human questions that take years to answer, while the Soo left me behind. I had to follow."

Hush reached over and touched her shoulder. "I did not want to give you fear," he said softly. "But who has the Soo is not gentle. He is not afraid to kill."

Puck shuddered. There were two killers on board. "I've got something I'd better tell you," she said, and revealed to Hush what she had seen that night on the station docks, and the conversation she'd heard between Leesa Sigmund and Mizzer Cubuk.

"When I met him, Mizzer Cubuk was kindness," Hush murmured sadly. 'I heard you had a something stolen,' he said to me. 'Bad luck. I hope they get it back for you.' I had so much happy that someone cared, I described its beauty to him. Now I am thinking he is finding it for himself and was wanting to know what it looked like."

"So what part does the captain play in all this, do you think?" Puck asked. "She's obviously soft on Cubuk."

Hush shook his head. "Not partners with Cubuk, I am thinking. A friend of your bearded man, perhaps, and Cubuk making nice to her to find her hiding place? Or maybe innocent."

"She asked me to make friends with you." Puck squirmed as she admitted this. "Not that I wouldn't have anyway," she added hastily. "But do you think she did that so you'd have a kid in your way to slow you down?"

"I have not the knowing," he said. "But it is her ship the Soo is hidden on. Without the knowing of what is real, it is better not to say a word to any human. I am still alone in this."

Puck grabbed his hand. "No, you're not. You've got me. We've got a finder; Cubuk doesn't."

Hush seemed to brighten at that. "Yes. And the thieves will think me given up, while going home on the same ship that hides the Soo. That must be humor to them, you think?" His throat tightened momentarily. "But no one must see me search, or they may have a guess I know it is near and guard it more."

"I told you I could help," Puck said. "The thieves won't be watching me."

"But Cubuk is," Hush said.

Puck fell silent.

"It is late," Hush said. "Go to sleep, young one, and I will be thinking about this helping you offer."

Puck rubbed her eyes and got to her feet. "I don't care about Cubuk," she said. "You're my friend."

—

Who had hidden the Soo on *Cat's Cradle*? Puck wondered. One of the crew or one of the passengers? Had any of them been on Chiron when the Soo was held up for all to see? At breakfast she began her inquiries.

"Did you and your husband come up from Earth?" Puck asked Leesa Sigmund.

"Well, he did," the young woman answered. "I came in

from Chiron, where I was visiting my father. I met him on station."

Aha, Puck thought.

Loki Sigmund joined them. He bent to peck his wife's cheek. "Hello, youngling," he said to Puck. "Been keeping my sweet wife company, I see."

Leesa nudged him playfully with her elbow. She didn't seem the type to go creeping about at night up to no good.

On the way to the lounge Puck ran into Michael. "What are you doing?" she asked, hoping he had time to spare her.

"Delivering something to the bridge," he answered. He waved a light-board at her. "I've got to download an assignment to Owen's board so that he can grade me."

"I'll wait for the lift with you," Puck said, joining him. "How long was *Cat's Cradle* in port before we boarded her?"

"Three days. We came in Saturday."

Puck thought for a second. The Soo was stolen Friday. So it couldn't have been a crew member who stole it unless . . . "Got any new crew members?" she asked.

Michael laughed. "What's with all the questions?"

Puck quickly groped for an excuse. She remembered how Naima would write in a diary each night. "It's for my journal," she told Michael. "Maybe I'll want to work on a spaceship one day."

Michael grinned at her teasingly, and his almond-shaped eyes glittered. "I think you've got some time to go before you meet the minimum age requirement, and if there's a height limit, I'm not sure you'll ever make it."

"Thanks a lot," she said, and turned her back on him, pretending to be annoyed.

Michael tried to mollify her, exactly as she'd hoped. "Okay, okay. We've just hired on two new crew members for this trip."

She turned back in triumph. "Who . . ."

But the lift doors opened. "Gotta go," Michael said. "See you later."

She sighed. Maybe if she were a few years older, he wouldn't be in such a hurry.

The ladies were in the lounge playing cards for music chips. Mz Dante had quite a pile in front of her already, but Mz Florette seemed blithely indifferent to losing as she fluttered her cards down willy-nilly. Apparently the stories Leesa Sigmund had read about Mz Dante and gambling were more than rumors.

"Hello, my dear," Mz Florette trilled as Puck joined them. "How are you today?"

Puck shifted uncomfortably from one foot to the other; she still wasn't used to the woman's odd face, but she tried not to show that. "Bored," she admitted. "There's nothing much to do."

"Watch a vid," Mz Dante said, and Puck found herself smiling despite her nervousness.

"One of yours?" she asked.

Mz Dante beamed back at Puck, her angular, lined face

suddenly looking much younger. "Those old things? They wouldn't have them outside of a museum."

Puck was glad she didn't have to lie to butter the woman up. "I think they're great."

"What a lovely child you are for saying so," Mz Dante answered as she elegantly laid down another winning hand.

"Absolute zero," Puck said. "I bet you'd be a genius in the casinos on Chiron. Have you been there?"

"Why, yes, many times," Mz Dante answered. "Just recently in fact."

Well, that hadn't narrowed the suspects down at all, Puck thought. "Can I watch?" she asked sitting down beside Mz Dante on the couch. "How come you don't use money?"

Mz Florette giggled. "If we did, she would not be winning."

Mz Dante shot her friend an annoyed glance.

Hush came into the lounge, bowed toward the ladies, then settled himself in another couch.

"Shall we teach the child poker?" Mz Florette asked.

"What an excellent idea," answered Mz Dante.

It sounded like an intriguing prospect, but she'd never be able to concentrate right now. "I'd love to learn, but I just remembered something I wanted to tell Hush."

"Who?" said Mz Dante. "Oh, him." She frowned. "I shouldn't become too friendly if I were you."

"Well, you're *not* me," Puck snapped before she could help it, and turned away, her face burning.

"Oooh, that Mz Dante makes me mad," she said, plopping down beside Hush.

"It is the round one that makes for me uncomfortableness," Hush answered.

Puck giggled.

"Tonight is the first jump," Hush said.

"It is?" Puck's voice squeaked with surprise, and her stomach tightened with anticipation. She hadn't realized that their first jump through hyperspace was coming up so fast.

"Nights are being a good time to search," Hush continued. "A night when we jump is very better. All will be strapped in, except those with busyness on the bridge."

"I'll help," she said.

Hush held up his hands. "No. You must have safeness in bed. I will not be far," he reassured her when she protested. "I am feeling the signal on the passenger deck. It fades in and out, but it is there. When I have the knowing of where the Soo is, we will plan together the how of getting it."

He wasn't excluding her completely. That made her feel better. They would rescue the Soo together and hide it until they reached Shoon.

But she wished he weren't going out tonight alone.

CHAPTER
TWELVE

I can't believe I'm really going to do this myself, Puck thought. *There should be some ritual, some dance or song, something to celebrate the whole mystery of it.*

The lights dimmed as the ship drew power for the jump, and there was an almost imperceptible thickening of the air. Her chest tightened under pressure, then suddenly she felt light, light, light. Her grafix-screen wobbled like a flying saucer, and she grabbed her stylus as it floated by her nose. Weightlessness. An almost forgotten queasiness rippled through her stomach as she slid her drawing tools under the strap that held her.

She thought about the trip to Moonstation when she was five years old—an ordinary flight in real space. Her parents had a new assignment, and she was going with them. It was before the days when local shuttle rides had shipboard gravity, and she had huddled miserably in Dad's lap with her stomach rolling over the way it did when she'd spun too long on the merry-go-round.

"You won't feel sick long, Imp," he'd said in his light-brown voice. "It's only the first few minutes."

"Goodfellows are great free-fallers," chimed in her mother, then laughed at her alliteration, and turned the phrase into a song, which they all sang until tummy upsets were forgotten.

They'd played a game with her. Strapped in for leverage, they gently tossed her back and forth between their couches, and she shrieked with laughter as she spun a slow dance through the air.

"Goodfellows are great free-fallers," Puck sang softly to herself. Suddenly she was more excited than she'd dared allow herself to be until now. She belonged here. Despite her failures, she was her parents' child. The exhilaration even drowned out her anger at being denied this for so long.

The dim, quiet cabin felt as still as nights on Earth when snow lay thick on the ground outside, but how could she sleep when Hush was out there searching?

Then she heard something—a faint whisper, a growing murmur of an unknown tide coming in.

The lights faded even more, like a handlight dying, then a distant moan began. Her heart crawled to her throat. *Maybe this always happens in the jump*, she thought. But the noise sank and rose and babbled, as if a discontented crowd muttered outside. A crowd of what?

Puck stared at the door. It was a strong door, a safe door; she begged it not to open. Stupid, she told herself. There's an explanation. I'm just too dumb to know it. She hid under the covers.

But then she heard a cry—a solid cry—a voice she recognized. Hush!

Part of her said, *You didn't really hear anything. Those noises are playing tricks on your ears.* But she pictured Hush crumpled on the corridor floor, as terrified as Leesa Sigmund had been. He was a friend, and he needed her.

She unsnapped the harness with reluctant fingers. Her grafix-screen and stylus floated heedlessly toward the ceiling, and her comforter, anchored by her behind, curled upward, eager to follow. Thank heavens her loose sleepshirt and leggings wouldn't impede her.

She slid to the edge of the couch and hoped moving weightlessly was like riding a bicycle, never forgotten. Carefully she pushed off toward the door and gently thumped against it with satisfying accuracy. She held on to the door frame, building nerve for the next move.

"Puck!" Her name echoed from the corridor in a peal of fear.

She pressed the door pad gently; a slap would have boomeranged her backward across the cabin.

Outside was black. The dim light from the room cut no farther into the darkness than car lights in thick fog. The air hummed. *God, there's nothing to hold on to,* she thought, looking at the slick featurelessness of the corridor wall near her door. *I'll have to swim blind.*

The hum picked up to a rushing moan again. *It's only sounds,* she told herself. *It's part of the jump. I'm not the sort that goes crazy.*

"Hush! Where are you?" Her harsh cry cut through the air with comforting reality.

"Here," his trembling voice answered from her right.

"I'm coming, Hush," she called. *Jeez, I'm just a kid,* she thought as she kicked her legs, launching herself into the dark. *I don't want to go.*

Wisps of air flickered across her face as if something moved in the dark around her. *Just don't let anything touch me,* she prayed. *I couldn't stand it.*

"I'm coming," she called again to keep up her nerve.

She propelled herself around the corridor in a combination of kicks and careful pushes off the walls. To her relief she touched nothing else as she swam through a dark that might as well be the blackness between the stars.

Something whooshed behind her—maybe a door. She didn't dare turn, because the action would fling her out of control. The babble rose again, surrounding her. Moans flowered out of its confusion.

Then a chorus of howls split the din. A startled voice near its source spat a guttural oath, and her heart thumped hard. A clattering rang up the corridor. Something coming, fast. There was nowhere to hide. She didn't dare move. Then something barreled into her.

For a moment she tangled with a large, dense body, too solid to be a ghost, and smelling of sweat. Her finger caught in a hard loop, then came away. Whoever she wrestled with swore again in a language she didn't know. A light, ringing, metallic sound skipped across the wall, and Puck was sent flying, turning out of control down the corridor. She crashed into the wall and ricocheted off, the wind knocked out of her. Something smashed into the wall across from her, and she heard the rhythmic thudding of someone used to fast, weightless travel using alternate walls to shoot himself down the hallway. The disembodied cries seemed to follow it.

Don't flail, Puck told herself frantically, trying to control her flight. *There's equal and opposite reaction.* Her breath came in sharp little pants.

"Puck. Where are you going?" Hush called. He thought it was she that passed him.

Puck didn't dare answer until she'd slowed herself. Carefully, using her arms as rudders, she corrected her haphazard tumble to a slow glide. Ahead she heard the whoosh of large doors, maybe the freight lift. "Hush, that wasn't me."

"But what . . . ?" His voice was close. She used it to find him.

She was almost there when the lights came up slightly, illuminating the corridor in eerie twilight. They revealed a cabin door close by. She padded along the wall and clung to the barely raised metal frame.

Ahead she saw Hush, crouched on the floor, anchoring himself by a hand that gripped torn carpet. His eyes were big as headlights, and he clutched his face with the other disbelieving hand, as past her, past him, in the half-light, streamed a transparent flow of creatures—milky outlines in the air, with spindly legs, and double-jointed arms spidering from tattered robes. Sucked like smoke to a vent, one by one they disappeared into the crack of the freight-lift door: flattening, distorting, escaping, following. Their arms strained forward, groping, reaching, and, as they flowed by, she saw Hush's long gray face echoed in the wavering mist, but gaunter, more frightened, lost.

His people? How could that be? She shuddered at the alien, inconceivable sight.

Was Hush doing it? Was this created from his fear? She wasn't on Earth now; anything could happen. The universe expanded in an explosion of possibilities. Like the concept of infinity, it threatened to engulf her.

No. She anchored herself in reality. It wasn't Hush's doing, he was as aghast as she was.

The last vague figure reached the lift, swirled like a dead leaf in the wind, and was gone.

The faces, the poor faces. She could still see them in her mind, and it was sadness she felt, not fear.

Hush drifted, crouched into a ball, with his long arms curled over his head as if denying what he had seen.

"Hush, it's okay. They've gone." She pushed off, floated to him, and put her arms around his shoulders.

He lifted his head to meet her eyes. She saw he clutched the pendant at his neck. "So is the Soo," he said. "I don't feel it anymore."

CHAPTER
THIRTEEN

They sat in Hush's cabin, sharing the strap of his sleep couch to keep from floating.

Hush bowed his head. "The finder is not working. Something blocks it. I will never have the finding of the Soo now."

"But how? What?"

"We have had the seeing of what, I am thinking," he said, raising his solemn face to look at her. "They make a disturb in the air, and interfere."

"What are they?" Puck asked.

"We had a talking about names when first friends," Hush reminded her, "and I said of a person named with a hero's name."

"Yes," Puck answered. "But you said we don't always become our names, and he died young."

Hush nodded. "He did, and this is the tale of his dying. This person's name was Wheywa'shoonyashanyaha." Hush touched the first of his three fingers to his nose. "He was my ancestor, and of the same birth-parent as that unhappy keeper who carried the Soo, the Child of the Asha, off-world.

"Whey traveled to live in another village to have the nearness of a great teacher. Our family smiled, because he used wisdom well. He could cure the ills of animals, and already farmers offered him food for advice. Always he had a creature with him to love.

"Then Grakk in breathing masks came up from the south, their squat forms dancing light in our gravity. They were hunters of knowledge from the stars, they had told those who ruled the land, and held out their own knowledge in gift for ours. Our people find honor in such quests, and the council gave Grakk freedom to make visit to the places of learning.

"In the northern villages Grakk had many talkings with the elders, gave amusing presents, enjoyed our food, and took many notes. They made much praise of Whey's teacher, sharing his classes, and studying his stories. Finally they set up tall markers, for surveying they said, but they were homing beacons.

"Airboats came down to each village. Those that would not march into an airboat were burned into stinking lumps. The Grakk took whole settlements—adult and child—up to a waiting mother ship, and left soldiers in exchange. When the rulers of Shoon found what happened, thousands and thousands were gone, and nowhere was Shoowa enough to be making an army to fight them. The left-behind people became servants on a new Grakk military outpost."

"What about Whey?" Puck asked.

Hush's elongated fingers knit and reknit.

"Whey was made captured like the many others were.

He tried to make free the little pet ook he kept in his shirt, but the soldier who pushed them crushed the creature under his boot. It didn't have the know-enough to run away."

Puck got an aching lump in her throat that she couldn't swallow away. "Why would he do such a thing?"

Hush held out a palm to her, as if his explanation rested there. "The Grakk have a hate of little creatures since a long-time-ago bad plague spread by animals. It is not much of a sorry."

Puck doubted that even Cubuk could be so mean. "What did Whey do?" she asked.

"Whey could not have the doing of anything." Hush curled his fingers tightly. "He was struck most brutal into the face when he cried his voice in sorrow, and hurried on with kicks. On the mother ship brother was torn from sister, parent from child, and chained to different walls in decks apart so aloneness would make them weak."

Puck remembered how Hush had quailed at the sight of the chain in the hold. No wonder.

"The gravity was too heavy, the air pumped in was not good air, and the Grakk gave no mouth filters. To the Grakk this was sense. The Shoowa chests hurt with the trying to breathe; Shoowa limbs ached with the trying to move. No Shoowa could fight.

"It got worse to worse.

"When the ship made the returning to its dockworld,

the captain gave the blame of what happened to simple error."

"Blame of what?" Puck whispered, afraid to know.

"Some creature," Hush spat, startling Puck. "Some Grakk, making repair, moved air ducts and made meetings wrong. Grakk air flowed into Whey's hold, and twelve hundred Shoowa died in poison."

Puck couldn't suppress her gasp of dismay, but Hush didn't hear, his eyes looked into the past. "The Grakk tossed the bodies into space like garbage. No words were spoken to the creator. No thing was done to set them free from the universe.

"The other prisoners told of this great sadness parent-to-child, and that ship will for always be a night terror to all exiled Shoowa. It is a death ship."

A cold realization gripped Puck, and Hush saw it on her face. "It is this ship," he said, confirming her fear.

Puck's flesh crawled. She'd known the ship was war loot, but this was worse. "I'm on a bemmie slave ship," she whispered.

"It was in a yesterday," Hush said sadly. "Nothing is remaining but memory."

"More than memory," she said. "I saw them, Hush. I saw people like you."

"Another shape of memory," he replied calmly, but she'd seen the fear on his face. He kept it from his voice now, however. "When a creature meets death suddenly, in fear and great hurt, sometimes there is a shock to the . . .

to the . . ." He tapped the thumbs of his right hand together as he groped for a term. "Center of life—what makes one creature different from another."

"The soul?" she suggested.

"Hai, we name it. The Hai or soul was not ready for a journey and has no believing in the body as dead. It is trapped in the place of death and can do nothing but relive the sorrow, pain, and fear."

"They're what we call ghosts," Puck said sadly, remembering the heart-breaking faces of the fleeing creatures.

"Then you are people, too," Hush said, as if he'd doubted up till then, "for you have Hai."

Puck reached for his hand. It was warm and dry. He matched her grip, and she felt safer.

"They are not to fear." Hush was reassuring himself as much as her, she knew. "They are much sadness. I have such anger that this could happen. They are trapped."

"Could the ghosts be untrapped?" Puck asked.

Hush looked surprised. "I have heard tales," he said. "If the trapped Hai are led away from the prison, it will break the tie and they will have free."

Puck sighed. They were on a spaceship. There was nowhere to go. "How could they be led?" she asked anyway.

Hush rubbed his forehead with bony knuckles. "Perhaps the way is a different each time. I am remembering the tale of a Hai who followed his life-mate to freedom, and another of a child who led the Hai of his mother from a cave out to mountain sky with her loved little ook, when she would not follow him alone."

"So, something the ghosts care about deeply could free them," Puck said. Suddenly she gasped. "We know what they'll follow, because they just did."

Hush held a questioning palm out to her. "They did?"

"Sure," Puck said. "Someone knocked me aside and went down the freight lift, the ghosts followed after, and then you couldn't sense the Soo anymore."

"Ohwo," Hush said, and stroked his face thoughtfully.

"Now it's twice as important to find the Soo," Puck said. "When we take the Soo home, we can also take the ghosts home and free them, but . . ." She paused. "How in the heavens will we manage that?"

"We will have to eat that meal when we are served it," Hush said, and Puck knew he wasn't going to give up after all.

She laughed.

"You find humor?" he asked.

Puck shook her head ruefully. "We haven't even solved the first problem, and I'm worrying about the next one. I must be an idiot."

"No," Hush said, wiggling an impossible finger at her. "Only kindness. Very much kindness."

CHAPTER
FOURTEEN

Puck slouched in a cozy-chair in the empty lounge, examining a small golden hoop earring. On the way to breakfast she'd searched the corridor for anything that could be the object she'd torn loose from the unknown villain. This was what she'd found wedged between the carpet and the wall. Was it a clue or just a coincidence?

Had Cubuk taken the Soo from the passenger deck last night, she wondered, or the original thief? Cubuk was lean and muscular and acted as if he were familiar with space travel. She bet he would have no trouble maneuvering in weightlessness.

"Daydreaming?" came a chiding voice.

"Michael!" She blushed, and shoved the earring into a pocket.

"You can't possibly be bored," he said with a grin.

"Well, yes and no. What's recent?"

"You mean aside from going through H-space into another part of the galaxy and getting ready to orbit an alien world?"

"Okay, okay." Then what he'd said sunk in. "Is this a stop?"

Michael sat beside her. "Yeah. Epsilon Eridani Four. Jackpot, the colonists call it."

"Oh, yeah." Puck said casually, but underneath she was panicked. "Is anyone getting off?"

Michael frowned. "As far as I know, we're only unloading equipment and supplies."

I've got to talk to Hush, she thought. *We've got to use the finder on everything that goes down.* "Can I watch?" she asked.

Michael obviously thought it was a strange request. "I don't see why not. I'll check."

"Hush too?" she added.

"Yeah, yeah. I guess you're genetically predisposed to the study of aliens, huh?"

His joke irritated her. Couldn't he see friendship as a possibility? She changed the subject. "Hey, how was the jump? Did you get to navigate?"

"I got to observe as usual," Michael said. "Maybe next time." Puck noticed he didn't look too eager. "But if hyperspace doesn't drive me nuts, Owen will."

Puck smiled. "How come?"

"Well, he hardly ever talks to me, you know—aside from lessons, that is. Then this morning, after the jump, he takes me aside and says, 'We've got ghosts.' "

"Ghosts!" Puck exclaimed.

Michael rolled his eyes. "Yeah. What a loon. 'I thought you might have noticed,' he said, 'since you're sensitive enough to see in hyperspace.' 'Not me,' I told him. He looked real disappointed, so I felt kinda bad. 'Maybe it's just void sickness,' he said."

"Weird," Puck said aloud, but now she knew why Owen had been so upset by Hush.

Michael yawned. "Not enough sleep and too much to do. Gotta run. I'll send you a com about the unloading, okay?"

He's a good sort, she thought as she watched him leave. She wondered if she dare tell him about the Soo.

Mz Florette wafted in then, wearing a hideous flowered scarf piled around her head like a turban. Puck stifled a giggle and left quickly for her room.

—

Puck and Hush stood on the main cargo level and observed as half a dozen workers in protective pad-suits brought crates up from below in the freight lift and loaded them onto hover-skids, uttering grunts and frequent cheerful curses. Sometimes they unloaded from both sides of the lift at once to double the speed.

The inner and outer cargo doors were open, and the ship's airlock was joined by accordion tube to a warehouse dock that could have been anywhere. The tube was on localized null-grav, and suited dock workers guided the floating freight across with long hooked poles. Mizzer Ernest wove in and out of the airlock on a hovercycle, directing the work.

Puck and Hush tried to sneak as close as possible without getting in anyone's way.

In one of the bays sat a squat gray escape pod. Tracks

curved from the pod's bay around to the airlock doors to position the craft for takeoff. Hush drifted over there with seemingly casual interest, but Puck could see the straining in his throat. Every so often he stretched out a long, knobby finger and touched a joint or surface. His other hand held the pendant. She saw him reach up into a vent in the nose and wondered if that would help him feel around inside. He shook his head and frowned, and she knew he sensed nothing.

The deck was momentarily empty as crew floated freight out the doors and others went down on the lift for more. An unaccompanied man came in from the airlock, and she backed into a bay out of his sight. Hush was on the other side of the escape pod by now, so the man thought he was alone. She watched him open a door with a triangle symbol on it in the ship's core and reveal a closet hung with padded overalls. Puck tensed. If he pulled out anything resembling a statue, she'd tackle him and scream for Hush as loudly as she could.

But he only ripped off some pads that were heavy-Velcroed to the inside of the door, stuck them to his knees, and went back to work. Puck had to sit down and take deep breaths to calm herself.

Hush crouched beside her. "Are you seeing something?"

"Just some man getting extra padding," she answered. "How about you?"

"I am not feeling it," Hush said. His high forehead was creased into more wrinkles than even he usually had.

"That's good, isn't it?" she asked.

"If the finder is working," he answered.

"All we can do is trust it," she said, leaning back against a bulkhead.

He sighed. "You are wise." Then a moment later he clenched his fists. "But what if I am feeling it go? What then?" His voice grew more intense. "I will become sick, crazy. I will get off the ship any way I can. I will have to follow."

Puck patted his arm in sympathy. She, too, dreaded this possibility.

"Look," Hush said.

Mizzer Cubuk strolled around the core of the ship. He stopped, hands on hips, and watched the unloading.

Puck scooted farther back into the bay, tugging Hush to come with her so they wouldn't be noticed. "See his earring," she said, and told Hush about the earring she had discovered in the corridor. "I'm sure that was him last night. He found the Soo and he's shipping it down."

Hush shifted from one foot to the other nervously. "Let us move nearer the doors," he said. "Maybe I am being too far away."

"Wait," Puck said. There was an argument going on by the freight lift. She peeked out at Cubuk. He'd noticed the argument too. Surprise, then worry, crossed his face.

A burly man was giving the little weasely guy who

106

worked in the galley a hard time. He kept his voice low, but sneered nastily as he jabbed his finger at the crate that sat on a floater between them. The Weasel's hands were balled, but held close to his sides in check. "So, big deal. I'll take it down again," he said loudly in a high-pitched voice, and called the lift sharply.

Cubuk looked relieved.

"Why do they argue?" Hush asked.

Puck cocked her head. "That crate wasn't supposed to be unloaded. Did you see Cubuk's face?" she asked then. "I was wrong about him. He's here for the same reason we are, to make sure the Soo *isn't* shipped down. We've got to look in that box. I think that's his hiding place."

Hush nodded excitedly. "I see. I see." Then his face fell. "It will seem strangeness if I go fast there to feel it with my finder."

"You don't have to," Puck said. "We'll check it out down on the freight deck."

"But down below, the crates look all the same. How will we have knowing which one if the finder will not work?"

Just then Mizzer Ernest swooped in on his scooter. "You there," he called to the men at the lift. "Stop lollygagging." And he zipped on out again.

The big guy went back to work, but not before giving the Weasel one more threatening glare.

"Quick," Puck said, getting up. "Go talk to Cubuk. Distract him." She gave Hush a gentle shove.

Puck hurried toward the lift, searching frantically in her

pockets for something to mark the crate—something not obvious. A big red *X* was definitely not the way to go. Her left hand found something warm and sticky in an inner breast pocket. Wrinkling her nose, she drew it out. It was melted chocolate left over from yesterday.

She was about to swoop up some stray packing material to wipe it off, when she had an idea. Instead she kneaded the gooey wrapping in her hand and wiped a smear on her upper lip for good measure. Hush was planted squarely in front of Cubuk, blocking his view. She saw him shift as Cubuk tried to look past him. Thank goodness that Shoowa caught on fast.

"Hey," she said, coming up behind the Weasel. He turned a startled face toward her. "Going up?"

"No, down," he snarled. "And you're supposed to use the passenger lift."

"What's this?" she said, slapping the side of the crate.

"None of your business," he snapped as the lift doors opened. When he maneuvered the floater into the lift, Puck was pleased to see a perfect chocolate handprint on the crate. Even if someone saw it, they wouldn't think she'd done it on purpose.

"Hi, Mizzer Cubuk. Isn't this great?" she called as she approached. "Come on, Hush, let's find a game to play in the lounge."

Let Cubuk think I'm a dumb kid, she thought as she linked arms with the alien to draw him away.

CHAPTER
FIFTEEN

Hush had an invitation to join the captain for dinner in her cabin that night.

"Maybe she's keeping an eye on you in case you suspect something. I bet she doesn't know Cubuk's got the Soo now."

"Maybe she is knowing nothing of the Soo at all," Hush said. He had a point, but they couldn't count on it. "But I am wishing to have a look for that crate soon. Mizzer Cubuk may be thinking his hiding place unsafe, too easily moved."

Yes, Puck thought. Cubuk might hide the Soo somewhere else. "I'll go while you're at dinner," she said, wishing she didn't have to.

"No." Puck could tell Hush was agitated by the way his fingers tangled among themselves.

"Look," she said. "Anyone who's keeping an eye on you will think you're occupied. No one will expect a grown-up to send a kid to do his work."

Hush sighed. "Then this must be a thing where humans have more sense than Shoowa," he said, and Puck knew she had won.

"I'll be careful," she said. There was no way she'd let

Cubuk catch her. No way at all. "Why don't you lend me the finder? It might make things faster."

"Ah, if I could," Hush said, shaking his head.

"But you don't know it's broken," Puck protested.

He waved his hands. "It is not that. It is that it is attuned to a Shoowa brain. You have a human brain. It will not work."

"Oh!" Puck was disappointed. "I guess you'll have to draw me a picture, then, so I know what I'm looking for." She handed him her grafix-screen.

Hush took only a few minutes to master the controls, then he created a picture of the Soo.

The Soo looked similar to a school sports trophy, Puck thought, but much more abstract. It was elongated, like Hush, and seemed to consist of airy filaments that wound and joined and shot skyward.

"Isn't it fragile?" she asked.

"No. Very, very strong," he answered. "Strong as our will to survive. Deceptive, as we have often had to be. It is our souls joining and reaching for freedom."

She wasn't sure she quite understood that. "How big is it?"

He looked at her carefully. "From your elbow to your fingertips, and not much wider than your arm."

"It looks strange," Puck said, slowly rotating the image on the screen so that she could see the back. "I can't follow the threads. Maybe you didn't draw it right."

"It is right," Hush answered. "It is having a mathematical magic."

Puck remembered when her math teacher, Mr. Perella, had taught them about Möbius strips—no matter what side of the twisted figure eight you started drawing a line, you ended up on the other side of the paper with no sane reason for being there. "Okay," she conceded, and printed a flat image small enough to carry in her hip pocket.

"It is a strange, yes," he said. "And most beautiful. The metal has a charge, and the twistings give life to a rainbow dance in the space between strands. It has the glimmer of life, the glowing of the soul. No computer construct can show that."

To Puck's surprise, at the door he took the finder from around his neck. "It will not work," he said seriously as he placed it around her neck. "But let it be my hearts to go with you."

"Yeah," Puck said, with a shaky smile. "It'll bring me luck." She tucked it inside her jumpsuit so that no one would ask questions.

Outside the lounge she ran into Leesa Sigmund.

"Robin," the woman cried. "Do you know where Michael is? We were told he was the person to ask if we needed anything." She flipped thick, pale locks back over her shoulders with a careless whisk of slim hands.

"Sorry," Puck said. "I haven't seen him since this morning."

"Oh, scuzz," Mz Sigmund said. "That Mz Florette's got a

tear in that hideous all-in-one thing of hers, and she wants a plasti-welder to mend it. It's driving me and Loki nuts listening to her complain."

"I'll find Michael and ask him to bring one, all right?" Puck told her. What a great excuse to explore, she thought. There was plenty of time until dinner.

Puck half turned to hit the lift again, but Mz Sigmund hadn't finished. "Let's get together, Robin," she said. "We could experiment with my makeup and have a chat. You have to let me know if you've picked up on any good gossip." She giggled, but her eyes were hard, and questioning.

"Maybe later, then," Puck said, but she felt uneasy.

Puck decided to check with Michael's tutor, Owen Swann. If Michael wasn't with him, she'd try the bridge.

She had butterflies in her stomach as she stepped out of the lift. She remembered from the tour that some crew members didn't like guests suddenly appearing on crew decks. Luckily the name of the occupant was posted on each door, and she soon found Swann's cabin. She knocked. There was a moment's silence, then a muffled voice said, "Come."

Activated by the voice, the door whisked open long enough for her to step into a chaotic room. There were stacks of black cubes everywhere, like the ones Swann had carried the first time she'd seen him. They were on the bed, on a worktable, and on the floor, where he sat with a couple more in his lap. They also lined the shelves of a large, built-in case with glass doors. Between the piles were small tools and other oddments: a sock, four empty coffee mugs, a shoe, calipers, some marbles set out in a wedge formation, a ceramic dinosaur, and a lamp shaped like the first hyperspace ship, *Orion*. Dreamlike music played so softly that Puck didn't notice it right away.

There were star charts all over the walls, except for the place reserved for a holo of the Horsehead Nebula. A brightly colored abstract design rose from the vidcom, and a cursor flashed on and off in the middle of it, waiting for a command. Puck was delighted.

Owen Swann looked up from the tools he was examining on the floor and blinked at her, owllike. "Yes?"

"Sorry, I was looking for Michael." Who was obviously not there, Puck noted.

"Umm, I think he's with Nast this hour," Swann said. He shifted slightly, and a *mrupp* of protest emerged from his lap. He moved the cubes there to reveal a little black-and-white cat.

"Podkayne," Puck said, surprised.

Swann smiled suddenly, like a child. "She loves a lap." He rubbed the cat's head affectionately. "And a scratch behind the ears."

Podkayne rumble-purred.

Puck knelt down with them and stroked Podkayne under her creamy chin. The cat purred even louder, if that was possible. *Owen's not bad,* Puck decided. *Strange, but nice.* She tugged at her coverall to get comfortable, and found the picture of the Soo escaping from her back pocket. She shoved it back in.

Thinking of drawings, she glanced again at the design that hovered over the grid of his vidcom. "Are you an artist?" she asked.

He raised his eyebrows, then realized what she was looking at. "Oh. No," he said. "It does look like some piece of art, doesn't it? But it's nothing compared with the real thing."

"What real thing?"

"Hyperspace, of course."

Puck stared at the image with even greater interest. "Is that what you see?"

"Well, partly," he answered.

"I heard everyone sees something different in hyperspace," Puck said.

Swann nodded. "So when you're teaching, all you can do is show someone the right way to go as you see it, and they have to remember what they saw. But there has to be a way of finding out those objects' relationship to realspace and charting it."

"Really?" Puck pointed at the vidcom. "And that's a map?"

He laughed softly. "Oh, no, that's just a sketch. Here's a map."

He held a black cube toward her, stroking a thumb along a lower corner. It lit up. Within the cube floated bright spirals, colored geometric shapes, and ribbons of stardust, all lit by an opalescent glow. The surface of the cube was etched with a more familiar star map that overlaid the bright carnival within. A hum came from the box, and she couldn't tell if it was meant to be music or only pleasant sounds. He turned the box, and the shapes changed in dramatic, unexpected ways. The noises beeped and quivered and changed too. One soft squeak made her feel such sudden pleasure that she moved to touch the box, and the feeling grew as her hand approached, making her grin uncontrollably.

"I've included a biostimulator," Owen said, seeing her reaction. "It works using sounds and pheromones. You see, there are feelings to add in. The things I see give me feelings."

"But how can you map feelings?"

"I listen to music or read poetry and note the passages that bring on the right feel. Then I fiddle with my kit until I get the right effect."

Puck hoped he wouldn't show her one that made him feel bad. "Are these all maps, then?" Puck asked, looking around.

"Yes," Swann said. "The ones shelved are done." He tumbled Podkayne off his lap, despite her protests, and hurried over to the glass case. He opened the door and began eagerly setting each cube ablaze with light and color.

Puck joined him in front of the display, absolutely enthralled by the magic scenes within—they were tiny starscapes from fairy universes, their sounds and feelings merging in a disturbing whirl. Puck found she was crying, but didn't know why.

Swann turned to say something and noticed her tears. "Whoops!" He closed the glass door, and a weight lifted from her. "Sorry," he said.

Now they could stand and look at the scenes without being affected by them. It took a moment for Puck to get over feeling flustered at her reaction.

"I can't believe it," she finally said. "It's amazing."

"I'm not sure how, but I know where I am in hyper-space," Swann said quietly. "I can sense the outside as well as the inside, and the thin points, the places where the universes are close. I'm drawn to those places, and going through feels like coming inside to the warmth on a rainy winter night. I open myself to it, and the right paths call to me, and the dangers scream beware. I'm trying to show what I see and feel in there and compare it to star charts to see if there is any correlation, anything that matches up. But even if I put together something I understand, maybe no one else will."

Puck was a little overwhelmed by his tumbling confidence. "Someone might understand," she said. "People understand art, and that comes straight out of someone else's head. And people understand real-space astronomy, and that's pretty hard to believe in, even when you know it's true—all those giant distances and impossible objects. This is like both."

Swann touched the glass in front of him thoughtfully.

"Thanks," he said. Then he seemed to pick up energy again. "Look," he said. He sat back down on the floor and picked up another cube. "This is our route this time."

Puck sat beside him as he lit the box up. "And no one but you can understand it," she said.

Owen grimaced wryly. "Once I showed one to a colleague who'd made the same run. She said it didn't look a thing like what she'd seen. Michael sees things differently too."

"How differently?" Puck asked.

"Different colors, shapes, everything. The mind of each individual interprets hyperspace into images that make the most sense to that person. As far as I know, only the Grakk ever see the same thing as each other. That's why they were able to develop it in the first place."

Swann turned the cube as he talked, staring into its depths. "It's hard to get people to talk about what they see, but I think humans see similar things more often than they admit, that's what makes me think there's a logic to it. I suspect a lot of navigators don't want maps because then more people could do our job and maybe we'd get paid less."

"It still wouldn't exactly be an overcrowded field," Puck said, "if you eliminate all the people who don't see anything, or throw up when they do." She gazed at the beautiful three-dimensional chart before her. "So, if there's no one else who wants to know about this or will understand, why do you bother?"

"For me," he said. "I feel if I put what I see in order, then my life will be based on logic, not on something strange that other people are scared of." He sighed, and was silent for a moment. "Anyway it's beautiful and should be shared."

Podkayne walked up his chest with her front paws and nudged at his chin with her face.

"Okay, Pod," he said, laughing, and lifted her back into his lap. "She thinks she's my mother," he explained.

Puck could tell he liked the idea of someone to look after him, even if it was a cat. *He must be lonely,* she thought. "So, do you get a chance to work on your charts much?" she asked.

"Much more lately," he said. "It's been nice and quiet." Then he blushed, and Puck guessed he was talking about the ghosts.

She decided to take a chance. "You haven't seen them the last few days, have you?"

His eyes opened wide, and she knew she was right.

"I think I know who they are," she said. "If you want to know."

"You see them too?" he said at last.

"Only once, when we were in hyperspace," she answered. "The other time I heard them."

"Yes, that's right," Swann said with growing excitement. "If anyone notices them, it's usually in hyperspace, but they pretend it's some quirk of perception caused by the jump and laugh it off. Michael hears things, too, but he

118

won't admit it. I think he's afraid of being thought another crazy hyper-jock. Podkayne doesn't need hyperspace to see them, do you, puss?" He kissed the cat's head. "Have you ever seen a cat stare at nothing, swishing her tail? Cats can see ghosts."

"And so can you," Puck said.

He nodded, and his mood changed once more. "They drift around looking so sad, I can't bear it. I'll turn a corner and there one will be, half in the wall, half out, and suddenly I'll want to burst into tears. Sometimes I'll see them in groups, fleeing down a corridor like clouds before a storm. I don't know what they're running from."

"They're unhappy," she said. "They need to be free." And she told him the story. She knew Hush wouldn't mind. Swann could see the ghosts and feel for them; he deserved to know. "If I find a way to set them free," she asked at the end, "would you help?"

"Yes," he said eagerly. "But how . . . ?"

He was interrupted by a knock at the door. He shrugged his shoulders and called out, "Come."

"What are you doing here?" asked a surprised Michael.

"Got a message for you," she answered. And her conversation with Owen Swann was at an end.

CHAPTER
SIXTEEN

When Puck set out for the freight deck, her timing was off. Beatrice Florette was heading for the passenger lift. The horrible turban was gone, and Mz Florette sported an even more horrible purple hairdo that clashed with her green earrings.

"Why, Robin, my dear! Going to dinner?"

"I already ate," Puck said. "I couldn't wait."

Mz Florette laughed. "Oh, to be a growing girl again."

It didn't look to Puck as if the woman had stopped growing.

"And I must thank you," the woman exclaimed. "You found that dear boy who brought the plasti-welder."

"Hey, s'all right," Puck mumbled. The lift door opened, but Mz Florette showed no sign of stepping in.

"Well, I've got to write to my grandmother," she said, improvising something an old lady could relate to.

"Of course." Mz. Florette still didn't get on the lift, so Puck was forced to retreat to her room until the woman had gone.

There was a faint high-pitched hum in the hold Puck didn't remember hearing there before, and the lighting was very dim. The captain apparently didn't waste power on this deck when no one was working. A quick look behind a triangle-marked door, however, turned up a handlight.

The hold was not as full as it could be, but still, mountains of crates sat in the cargo bays. *Come on,* Puck encouraged herself. *The crate has to be in front. That guy was in a hurry to get other work done. He'd park it quick, near the lift.* She shone a powerful beam into the storage bay directly opposite the nearest freight-lift doors. *If I were him, I'd have put it here,* she decided. Unless, of course, he'd gone out the back doors of the lift.

On the side of a crate to the left of the bay she saw mucky fingerprints. Blast off! That was it.

"Can I help you, young lady?"

Puck almost had heart failure. Her fist clasped the handlight rigidly to the front of her jumpsuit as she turned slowly. Behind her stood Cubuk, frowning.

She gulped. "I was exploring."

"You seem to be exploring a lot, young lady. It's not safe for small girls to be nosing around so much."

A coldness expanded in Puck's abdomen. She backed away from him. He took several steps forward.

"I must *really* encourage you to return to the guest quarters," he said, sounding as casual as a snake. "You're not supposed to be down here."

Fear made her strike back. "Neither are you," she snapped.

His blue eyes narrowed. "I've got good reasons for being here," he answered. "Reasons that don't concern you. So, if you breathe a single word to anyone about this, or what you saw at the spaceport, you're going to be really sorry. I haven't the patience to put up with curious little girls. Now, get your butt above."

Puck didn't move. She couldn't.

"Scat!" He raised a fist.

Puck turned and ran for the lift, yelling for it to open. As soon as the front doors closed, she ran to the back and whispered another command. She slapped an up-button to cancel the order, then darted out the partially opened back door. The lift gave a soft *whoosh* as it went up without her.

Hah! she thought. *I don't run that easily.* She switched off her handlight with trembling fingers and crept around the core, until she found a dark nook behind two large pipes that ran up to the ceiling. They hid her, but she could see between them. The faint hum in the air deepened into a drone.

Cubuk lingered in front of the crate. He was smiling. It wasn't an evil smile, she thought. That surprised her. He looked like a boy who was enjoying a private joke.

He shook his head. "There's too many things to keep an eye on around here," he muttered. "But at least the competition's on my turf now." He checked his wristie and headed for the lift himself.

What made the ship his turf? she wondered. Because he had the captain twisted around his little finger?

She was about to leave her hiding place when the shadows to the left of the bay changed shape. Puck eased back into her own shadows. Maybe the dim light was playing tricks on her eyes. But the shape kept moving. Then a handlight lit the darkness enough for Puck to see a slim figure with pale hair. Leesa Sigmund.

Mz Sigmund went straight to the chocolate-marked crate, opened the lid, and eagerly pulled out handful after handful of packing material. *I can't believe this,* Puck thought. *I'm almost there, and she gets it. Am I strong enough to grab the Soo from her and run?*

Puck dropped to the floor and slowly crept across the deck to the bulkhead on the right of the bay and peeked from behind it. Mz Sigmund pulled an assortment of boxes out of the crate, then she sat on the floor with the boxes arranged in front of her and began opening them.

The first contained a round, sparkly object. Puck didn't have any idea what it was, but Mz Sigmund's lips pursed in a little matching O of appreciation. She pulled something out of an inside pocket and held it over the orb—a magnifier, or some kind of analytical device. A dull-brown jar was in the second box, and a necklace in the third. They both got the treatment. Mz Sigmund raised the necklace up to her throat and peered down to admire it, obviously wishing she had a mirror.

Puck was in a crouching position, like a racer before the

starter's gun. Every time Mz Sigmund opened a box, Puck raised slightly, ready to dash out and grab the Soo. Each time it wasn't the Soo, she sank again, her heart beating rapidly with fright. Her legs were starting to ache.

What is all this stuff? Puck wondered. She was sure nothing there was the Soo, but she reached for the picture in her pocket to double-check anyway. The picture was gone. She must have dropped it somewhere. Oh, well, she decided, if anyone found it, they'd only think it was a doodle.

None of the next three items was the Soo either, but Mz Sigmund didn't seem to be worried. She was really happy with what she'd found. "Too many things to keep an eye on," Cubuk had said. Was the Soo only part of the loot he wanted to steal from his competition? Was he keeping an eye on the rest until the time was right?

It was amazing. These thieves seemed to spend as much time stealing from each other as they did stealing from innocent people.

Puck became aware that the drone that had been going on for some time was getting louder. They were only one deck up from Engineering—was it machines? No. It sounded more like a rising wind, except how could there be a wind in a hold?

Mz Sigmund must have heard the noise too. She glanced up nervously. Her eyes grew large as she gazed over Puck's head into the dark beyond. She looked as frightened as she had the other night in the corridor. It was then Puck realized what the sound was.

Now voices could be distinguished, rising above the drone, and the faint ceiling lights far above began to flicker. Mz Sigmund got to her feet, nearly dropping her handlight. She backed slowly away. Her heel caught on some packing; she almost tripped, her arms flailed. She turned and fled.

The loot lay abandoned on the floor.

The ghosts never hurt anyone, Puck was almost certain of that.

A shriek split the air.

CHAPTER
SEVENTEEN

Puck straightened up hesitantly. There was nothing there. No looming phantoms with outstretched claws. No distraught transparent visions. No ghosts.

But the sound of them echoed across the deck, and there was excitement in their voices this time, not anguish. Could they sense she was a friend ready to help them? Her hand went to the lump where her jumpsuit covered the finder. Or perhaps the nearness of something made by their people gave them hope.

They had flowed through the lift door following the Soo, and now they were gathered down here. Could the Soo be nearby after all?

Another sudden shriek made her flinch. If they were dangerous, Hush would have warned her, she reassured herself. But who knew what dead things would do?

The lights wavered like candle flames, and she made her way through the quivering shadows to where the noise was loudest, the bay opposite the far lift door. The howling was so fierce there, she had to hold her hands over her ears, but Puck stared in dismay. The bay was empty. She backed up one. There were a few crates in that bay, but the noise was less. It was the same on the other side: a few crates, but less noise. The Soo had to be where the ghosts were, but there was nothing there.

Puck spat out the nastiest word she could think of. She shone her handlight into every corner of the bay and found only gray metal walls traced with pipes, and one of those painted over Grakk logos the buffers had missed. At least the howls had subsided to a low hum again, and the lights steadied, as if the ghosts were satisfied that she was on the trail. They made Puck less nervous when they were quiet.

There was a light fixture above the bay and, nearer the back wall, an air vent. In the curve between wall and ceiling was a flower-shaped cog, probably a water sprinkler.

There was another, smaller, grill-covered vent near the bottom of the wall. As she watched, the grill bounced—and so did she. Her hand went to her heart.

"Mrrrrup!" The grill popped up, and Podkayne squeezed through like liquid fur. The little black-and-white cat wound around Puck's legs.

Puck sighed with relief. "Come to help?" she asked.

Wait a minute, she thought. If a cat could get behind the walls, there would be enough room for someone to hide something there.

She had to lie down flat on the floor before she could get an arm into the vent. Her body twisted this way and that as she groped around inside, but it was no good, she couldn't feel anything. She eyed the hole. No, she wasn't small enough to fit through. But what about the vent in the ceiling? She slipped her handlight into her pocket.

The pipes on the wall made excellent climbing, almost as good as the bars up the wall of the gym at school. But even hanging on to a pipe and stretching out as far as possible, she could only reach the vent with her fingertips. She didn't have enough leverage to push up.

She pulled herself back, sliding her hand along the ceiling to keep her balance. When her hand crossed the flower-shaped cog, it depressed slightly, and something rumbled beside her. She snatched herself aside, risking a fall. *What have I done?* she thought, and then saw a narrow gap had opened in the wall. A panel, so smoothly fitted to the surface she hadn't noticed it, had moved ajar. It was marked as a door by a two-inch stick figure impossible to see from the ground.

"Hey," she whispered, and reached for the cog again. This time she pressed firmly and the panel slid back all the way. She edged over and pulled herself through.

The panel closed automatically behind her, and she gasped in panic. *Calm down,* she thought, and pulled her handlight out and switched it on.

She was on a platform between the inner and outer hull of the ship. The walls were about a man's arm span apart, so there was plenty of room to move. A peculiar smell permeated the air, like that of the heating turned on for the first cold fall day. *Cubuk must really know ships to hide the Soo here. I wonder if space is right outside that wall,* she thought. It gave her a spooky but delicious feeling.

There was another rosette to the right of the panel, similar to the cog outside. She pressed it, and the panel opened once more. She felt much better the second time the panel closed.

The hum of the ghosts rose and fell like a distant storm at sea. Her light didn't penetrate far, but there was an echoing feeling to this place, and she knew it stretched far around the ship, following the circle of the deck. Who knew how many cargo bays led to platforms like this? Maybe all of them.

Through the grate of the platform she could see rungs leading down the inner hull that swelled out below. More rungs went up from where she was, curving inward to follow the shape of the ceiling within. Each step had a tread to help boots grip.

Thick wires and pipes hatched the walls like hieroglyphics, sometimes narrowing the space between the hulls claustrophobically. Here and there an unintelligible digital display glowed green and eerie beyond the reach of her handlight. Struts joined the hulls at regular intervals. They looked too thin to be effective against any pressure, but she knew that whatever they were made of, they were strong.

A scratching below made her look in time to see Podkayne slink back through the vent onto a lower platform. The cat stared at thin air, her tail twitching slightly.

Cats can see ghosts, Owen had said. She carefully descended the steps on the bulging wall.

She shone her handlight this way and that, looking for signs of the Soo, and halfway down to the cat door she spotted something wedged behind some pipes on the outer shell—a long bundle of dark cloth. She hardly dared to believe her eyes.

Luckily the pipes were built out to within her reach if she stretched. She had to put her handlight between her teeth to free up a hand; then, holding on to the steps for dear life, she reached out as far as she could and managed to grasp a corner of cloth. Slowly she tugged the bundle from its resting place. *Don't slip, whatever you do,* she told herself. When it was almost free of the pipes, she took a chance. She gave one last tug toward her, let go the tail of cloth, and grabbed. She had it.

The blood rushed through her veins, and her heart pounded, but she cradled the gossamer-light bundle to her like a baby and pulled herself back up to the platform accompanied by the contented humming of the ghosts. Her jaws were aching by the time she took the handlight from her mouth.

On the platform she sat and balanced the light on her knees as she gently unwrapped the package in her lap with trembling hands. *Only enough to make sure,* she told herself. Podkayne found her just as a corner of chamois-soft cloth slid away to reveal shimmering filaments.

"Absolute zero!" Puck whispered.

She replaced the cloth and turned to open the way out, but as her fingers touched the release she heard voices. Cautiously she cracked the panel a little and stuck the handlight in the gap so that it couldn't close.

When she looked down, the breath caught in her throat. It was those crewmen—the same pair who'd had the argument over the crate. And it was the crate they were talking about now.

"Did you see those grubby hand marks on the side?" the skinny weasellike one said. "There's somethin' naggin' me about that."

"Well, nothing's missing," the big one answered, "but if I find out who pulled that lot out, they're going to be sorry."

The Weasel cringed away from his companion's meaty fists. "I don't understand," he whined. "How would anyone know it was aboard?"

"It doesn't help, having an idiot lug it around from place to place," the big guy said. "Maybe you got someone curious."

"Me?" the Weasel squeaked. "You're the one that near bust a gut chewin' me out."

Please don't remember me, Puck wished fervently. *Or the chocolate.*

"What bothers me," the big one said, "is why they left it all there, laid out like that."

The Weasel scratched his chin. "Maybe they heard us comin'?"

"But did you see anyone run off?"

"No."

"That's what I mean. It's like some kid not putting its toys away."

This made the Weasel frown thoughtfully. *Oh, yikes,* Puck thought.

"It gives me the creeps," the big man continued. "This whole ship gives me the creeps. We'd better move that crate, and keep an eye on it this time."

"What?" The Weasel didn't look keen.

"Yeah, you can forget bed," his partner said as if reading his mind. "We're staying down here the night and keeping watch. And every night from now on."

The Weasel groaned, and Puck almost did too. *What do I do now,* she thought. *I'll be stuck here all night.*

"Maybe we can get Ernest to pull a shift," the Weasel said.

At the mention of the second mate's name, Puck's mouth dropped open. Then she remembered the padded leg she'd caught a glimpse of in his cabin. It must have been one of these men, that's why he was so nervous. If Mizzer Ernest was involved, anyone could be.

The big man grabbed a handful of his companion's coverall and rocked him slowly back and forth. "We'll leave Ernest out of this. He got the stuff aboard, that's all we need him for. Anyhow, I don't trust him. He was down here with the captain yesterday—and they were laughing. They split pretty fast when they saw me."

The Weasel pushed at the big man's chest ineffectively. "It's her ship. She can be anywhere she wants. Just 'cus they were laughin' don't mean nothin'."

The big man spat past the Weasel's ear, making him flinch. "Yeah, well I don't fancy being swindled out of this little lot." He let go of the Weasel.

"We'll be in deep scuzz if somethin' happens and we arrive empty-handed," the Weasel said. "The boss'll be *real* happy to see us then."

Puck gently removed the handlight and allowed the panel to close. *What do I do now?* she wondered.

Podkayne chirruped as if answering her and wound around Puck's legs, but she didn't stay long. She scrambled onto the next step and began to climb upward with practiced ease.

Guess you're right, Puck thought, and got up quietly. She tucked the Soo inside the front of her jumpsuit and fastened the buttons up again as far as she could.

This looks scary, she thought as she watched the cat scale the inward curve of the ceiling and disappear into darkness. But she knew it couldn't be anywhere near as dangerous as going back the way she had come, so she took a deep breath and she followed the cat.

CHAPTER
EIGHTEEN

Puck edged up the wall carefully in case she crushed the Soo. The top of the bundle got in the way of her chin, so she had to lean her head uncomfortably, and her neck began to ache. She wished she could grip the rungs with both hands, but she needed one hand to hold her light.

The light didn't reach far, and the darkness beyond was frightening. *Could there really be rats?* she wondered. If she touched Podkayne by accident now, she'd probably have a heart attack. Her legs trembled with the effort of climbing.

The wall she scaled curled forward to form the ceiling of the deck below, leaving a dark, spoked crawl space between it and the floor of the deck above. The outer wall arched over into a canopy that blocked access to the next level. Podkayne pushed herself through another cat door and left Puck staring up at the small grate.

"Brilliant! I can't get through that," she muttered.

She glanced down, biting her lip. But she couldn't go back. She scanned the barrier above, searching for signs of a door large enough for a human. The metal was seamless, and her neck hurt even more staring up at that angle. She needed a closer look.

As she reached up to get her elbow over the next rung, the Soo shifted and stuck her in the ribs, and her handlight began to slide out of her sweaty palm. She clamped the light to the closest surface, her face, hoping to catch it, but it shot from her fingers and crashed into the wall.

"Scuzz," she cried. She could hear its chaotic descent echoing up the ship. *Dumb. Really dumb,* she thought bitterly, holding her stinging cheek.

She crouched miserably over the rungs, afraid to move in case she slipped and followed the light. She was trapped at a dead end in total darkness.

She had almost stopped hearing the ghosts, but they sounded louder in the dark. Their voices seemed derisive. Suddenly she was angry at herself. "You're right," she said to the ghosts. "You've been trapped for generations. Why should I be sorry for myself?"

She adjusted the Soo to an almost comfortable position and thought hard. The crew had to get around to fix things. And no one could stand on that last rung she remembered seeing at the top of the ladder, unless they had headroom. So there must be a door. But where was the release?

She pretended she was a worker climbing up with tools. It would be hard to raise a hand above to the ceiling and keep one's balance, but what about forward?

She reached into the crawl space and felt gingerly between the ridges of a honeycomb pattern. Was there anything hazardous to touch—something "live"? No. They wouldn't let the cats run around if there was, but . . . ahh! Her fingers found a rough circle, and when she pushed, a draft blew down from above. To her relief, an expanding pale-green glow revealed an opening hatch. She climbed through and onto the platform above. She must be level with the passenger deck now.

Podkayne was nowhere in sight, but by the faint light of a bank of control buttons, Puck could make out the wall in front of her. It was marked with a stick figure, and she knew there was a way out.

What if I step right into someone's cabin? she worried. But more likely the exit would lead her into a maintenance room or something. Sure enough, when the panel whisked open, she stepped into a storeroom dimly lit by an emergency light over the door. Her lungs immediately felt bigger and full of fresh air.

She carefully maneuvered around a tentacled carpet cleaner and past shelves of fresh linens, to look out of the peephole in the door. There was no one about. "Shush!" she told the ghosts, as if that would help.

Outside, she scrunched her eyes up against the stinging bright light. Suddenly excitement bubbled to the surface. She'd done it! *Wait till I show Hush,* she thought gleefully, and almost skipped to his cabin door.

But he wasn't there, and she wanted to howl with frustration. She couldn't go find him; she didn't dare leave the Soo alone so soon after finding it. And if he was still with the captain, how would she explain dragging him away? It was torture.

She hurried back to her cabin before she could run into

someone drawn out by the gently moaning spirits of the Shoowa. As soon as she got in the door, she ran to the vidcom and left a message for Hush. She dared not be specific; the system wasn't secured. "Please come visit," she said, then added her name and hoped the sparseness of the message made him hurry.

It wasn't only eagerness to tell him that made her wish he'd come soon, she was nervous to be left alone with this thing Cubuk wanted so badly. She took the Soo to her couch and unwrapped it gently to have a closer look.

It was gorgeous. But try as she might, she couldn't make out the pattern the filaments weaved. The effort made her eyes prickle. She squeezed them shut and tried again, but it was no use. The colors shimmered, and the shapes evaded her. The Soo wasn't coldly beautiful, however. A warm feeling of well-being washed over her as she gazed at it, as if she, too, could feel the hope of the Shoowa. She realized from the quiet hum in the air that the ghosts were present, looking at the Soo with her.

She wrapped the Soo back up, along with the finder, and put them in the compartment under her couch, then spent most of the next hour pacing.

Finally there was a knock on the door.

"Hush?"

"It is," he answered, his voice vibrating with excitement. She opened the door.

"You have news?" he asked eagerly.

She laughed in delight. "Yes, yes." When the door

closed behind him, she danced to the couch, pulled the Soo from its hiding place, and put it, still wrapped, in his arms.

He hesitated as if he hardly dare believe, then gingerly began to unwrap. It was difficult to tell if his gray face lit up from joy or from the shifting colors of the treasure he revealed.

"Oh, my ancestors," he whispered. "Oh, stars. The precious child. How did this beautiful happening come to exist?"

And Puck told him.

"But we've got to hide it somewhere," she finished. "Because both the original thieves and Cubuk know it's yours, so you're the prime suspect for stealing it back if they find it gone." She paused. "You don't think anyone besides us has made the connection between the ghosts and the Soo, do you?"

Hush looked surprised. "Most unlikely." He gently sat the Soo beside her vidcom and thought for a moment. "But would it be making you feel better if we hid the Soo in a place that no one could get at even if they knew?"

"Where?"

"I am having an idea," he said. "But we must be asking Michael for help."

Puck was amazed. "Why Michael?"

"The most safest place on the ship is being under the hyperspace navigator's chair, protected by the force field.

Michael is apprentice. He has the power to put it there and no one knowing."

"But he's crew," she said. "We don't know who in the crew is involved. We might as well blow it all and ask Owen Swann himself if we're going to risk telling a crew member. At least he feels sympathy for the ghosts."

"But Michael is safer," Hush answered. "He is not all-the-time crew. Would Mizzer Ernest bare his belly to a student who is having no loyalty to him? Who is going back to school in short months?"

"Maybe not," Puck said. "But can we trust him not to run to the captain? He's big on her."

"Has he been anything but a friend to you?" Hush asked. "Has he given you reason not to trust?"

"Well, no," Puck admitted. And she did like him.

"We have to be trusting others sometimes," Hush said, "whatever humans have done in the before. I have trusted you, and that has been a worthy trust, I am thinking. It has given me braveness. Michael is another young human who I am feeling has honor. Let us be trusting him together."

"Okay," she said. "But only because you say so." She yawned. "It's late now. I won't be able to talk to Michael until tomorrow."

"Then I must be with the Soo all night?" Hush picked up his precious relic.

"You'll have to," Puck answered.

"I will not sleep," Hush said. But he didn't look disturbed by the thought. He glugged with happiness.

CHAPTER NINETEEN

There was something up the next morning. Everyone seemed to be on edge, or in a big hurry. The Weasel gave Puck the strangest look at breakfast, and missed her plate with the scrambled eggs he was dishing up; a young tech snapped at her when she stopped him to ask if he'd seen Michael; and even Mz Sigmund was arguing with her husband on the other side of the lounge.

It hadn't been too smart to run off and leave that stuff all over, Puck thought. Maybe that's what they were arguing about.

Mz Sigmund got up and came over, pulling her husband after her. Embarrassed, he rolled his eyes dramatically. *Uh-oh,* Puck thought.

"You heard it, didn't you?" Leesa Sigmund said, tossing her hair.

"Heard what?" Puck asked.

"That buzzing sound last night," Leesa said. "You know. Go on, tell him. He thinks I'm mad."

Hush thought it unlikely that anyone would make the connection between the Soo and the noises, but what if the wrong person did put two and two together? "What sound?"

"It doesn't matter," Loki Sigmund said, tugging at his wife's arm. "I believe you heard something."

Mz Sigmund wouldn't leave Puck alone, however. "But you did hear it that first night, you said so."

"Did I?"

"Let it go," Loki Sigmund said, leading his wife away. "We're on holiday, for Earth's sake."

"I won't," she answered. "There's a reason for those sounds, and I'll find it."

———

Puck found Michael in his cabin down on the engineering level.

"You're not supposed to be here," he said as he folded his sleeping quilt.

"I know." She sat down on a low stool. "But I need help." She bit her thumb and eyed him anxiously.

"You look serious," he said.

She hoped Hush was right about him. "You better sit down too," she said.

"Oh, no!" he responded, laughing. "Now I'm really worried." But he sat down on the edge of his couch.

Puck told him about the Soo: how it was stolen and how she'd found it again. Michael appeared doubtful at first, but her description of her climb up the exoskeleton of the ship convinced him.

"You're crazy," he said. "You could have been killed."

Puck shrugged. "It was safer than facing those smugglers."

"That big one's Sullivan," Michael told her. "The skinny man is Victor Zuzak, but 'the Weasel' suits him better. Remember when you asked me if we had any new crew members? Well, they just signed up on Earth Station. You think they took this Soo object?"

"Perhaps not personally," she said. "But they're mixed up in it, and so is Mizzer Ernest."

"So what about Cubuk?" Michael asked.

"I think he's part of a rival gang that's after their loot."

"And Leesa Sigmund?"

Puck shook her head. "I can't figure that one out."

"We've got to tell the captain," Michael said.

"Michael, what if she's in on the smuggling? Those men thought Ernest was double-crossing them with her."

Michael looked shocked. "Not Captain Cat."

"I don't like the idea either," Puck answered. "But it might be true. Please, Michael. Don't tell. It could ruin Hush's life and put us all in danger, when with only a little bit of help from you we can get the Soo home safely without getting her involved at all."

"Okay, okay," Michael said. "It's a long shot, but I admit there's the slightest possibility that she might be mixed up in this, so I'll wait to tell her about the smugglers and Cubuk until you and Hush have the Soo off-ship."

Puck didn't think it was wise that Michael *ever* mention

them to the captain, but she could wait to argue that point later. "So you'll do it, then?"

"Yeah, guess so. Where do you want to hide it?"

"Under the hyperspace navigator's chair."

"Puck!"

"Why not?" she asked. "Even if someone knows where it is, they can't get through the force field. It'll be safe."

"Well, I know I can give Owen a story to get the key," Michael admitted, "but if what you say is true, there'll be ghosts showing up, fast and furious. He'll go mad."

Puck could have kicked herself. Just because Owen knew who the ghosts were didn't mean they wouldn't upset him. He needed to know why they were there so that he wouldn't give everything away. They'd already taken a chance in telling Michael, now it was Puck's turn to ask Hush to trust someone.

—

Owen's eyes widened in surprise when he opened his cabin door and found Michael, Puck, and Hush standing there, but he invited them in. Puck sank to the floor to sit with Owen like she had before, and the others followed suit.

Hush placed the bundled Soo in front of them, and Owen inhaled sharply. He looked rapidly around the room and up at the ceiling. "You've got a lot of friends," he said, in a voice that trembled slightly, and Puck knew the ghosts had come too. "What's going on?"

Puck explained. ". . . And once we get the Soo down to Aurora, the ghosts will follow, I'm sure," she finished. "You wanted to help them."

Owen shook his head. "I'm truly sorry for all that's happened to you," he told Hush. "But the captain's a good woman. I'd feel like a traitor."

"That's how I felt," Michael joined in. "But if we can solve this ourselves, it can't hurt, can it?"

Owen wrapped his arms around his knees and held tight. "I need this job."

For the first time Hush spoke. "It is a fairness to you, I am thinking, to be showing you what you risk your honor for." And he began to unwrap the Soo.

As the shimmering filaments were gradually revealed, Owen's head came up, his grip relaxed, and a look of wonder came to his face. "It's got a song," he said, and Puck wished to creation she could hear it too.

Michael's mouth was parted in gentle surprise; maybe he felt the same surge of happiness she did.

"It's the colors of hyperspace," Owen continued, and Michael nodded. "Like the ripples right before you burst through to Lalande, skimming in the solar wind, or the rainbowed honeycombs the hyper-side of Sirius A." He sighed dreamily, then spoke to Hush in a firmer voice. "I understand how you feel. This is a thing of pure joy, and must never be violated."

Puck wanted to cheer.

Hush bowed his head, holding his arms out to Owen, hands in fists. "I am thanking you from great deepness."

Owen blushed. "Just the two of us can go," he said to Michael.

—

In a little over an hour Michael met Hush and Puck at her cabin. He was really wound up.

"The captain was in a meeting with Ernest and Nast," he said. "And everyone else was busy. No one noticed Owen and me hiding the Soo."

Hush fluttered his spindly fingers. "I am thanking you much. My hearts are quieter."

"Listen, I gotta go," Michael said. "There's a crew meeting—urgent."

"What's going on today?" Puck demanded. "Everyone's upset."

Michael hesitated. "I'm not supposed to say."

"You are being a friend to us," Hush said. "Do we have a need of knowing this?"

Michael rubbed nervously at the side of his face. "There's a crew member missing, one of your smugglers—Sullivan. He hasn't been seen since dinner last night."

"After dinner," Puck said. "I saw him." Her stomach knotted. "What could have happened to him?"

"I guess we'll soon find out," Michael answered. "We're forming search parties."

—

There was no trace of Michael's usual teasing smile when he came back to Puck's cabin later. "They found him," he said tersely as he sat down on her couch.

"Where?"

" 'Tween decks," he answered. "I'd say about where you found the Soo."

It left her short of breath. "And . . . ?"

"He's dead."

"How?" Puck gasped, trying to ignore the painful tightening in her chest.

"He was hit in the nose. The blow forced the bone into the brain. It killed him."

"That's how the servant on the space station was killed," Puck said. "The man whose uniform was stolen by the thief."

"It was the Grakks' favorite move in hand-to-hand combat during the war," Michael said. "Our troops picked it up after a while."

Puck remembered the swift and deadly way Cubuk had fought on the space station. "I bet Cubuk's a war veteran," she whispered.

"But he's the one who found the body," Michael said. Then he whistled softly in admiration. "That's a good cover. And it stopped anyone from finding any hidden contraband in there."

Puck wondered if Cubuk had had a good look around

inside, himself. "But why would he kill Sullivan?" she asked.

"Maybe Sullivan caught on that Cubuk was watching them."

"You don't think he'll kill Zuzak, too, do you?" Puck said.

Michael smiled ruefully. "Probably won't have to. The man's likely to be too scared to go near the loot now."

Puck agreed. No wonder the little man's hands shook so much when he was dishing up breakfast.

"But we've got to tell the captain about that contraband now," Michael said. "You should have seen her up on the bridge. She was really upset."

"Being upset doesn't make her innocent of smuggling," Puck said. "It only means someone's dead and she hasn't the foggiest idea who killed him."

Michael sighed. "I still can't believe she'd be in on this."

"Even if she's innocent, she's soppy for Cubuk. If you tell her, she won't believe you," Puck said.

"We don't have to tell her about Cubuk," Michael answered. "Just show her the valuables."

Puck flung her hands up in disgust. "Hey, if she isn't aware of that stuff already, I don't want to tell her. Cubuk saw me with that crate; he would know I told. I don't want a killer mad at me."

Michael screwed up his face in agony. He really admired Captain Cat. Puck understood how he felt. "So, got any other ideas?" she asked.

He sighed. "Get Hush off as soon as we dock over Aurora, and hand the whole thing over to the authorities. The port there is still in military hands. They can send troops aboard to confiscate the evidence. We only have to hold out until the day after tomorrow."

That seemed an age to Puck, and what would happen if Cubuk discovered the Soo was missing? She shivered.

Just then a familiar voice pierced the walls of her cabin with a mournful howl.

"Hush!" Puck cried.

They both raced to the door.

Two of the engineering crew were leading a slumped, shuffling Hush to the lift. Mizzer Nast followed. He glanced at them as the procession passed, and Puck was surprised to see he looked sorry.

"Protective custody," he said before she could ask.

"What does that mean?" Puck asked Michael.

Michael frowned. "Maybe they think he killed Sullivan."

"No!" Puck cried. She ran for the lift.

CHAPTER
TWENTY

"You have to understand," the captain said. "It's for his own protection. Mizzer Cubuk overheard some crew members saying ugly things."

Cubuk, Puck thought in disgust. It figured.

"And you know there are passengers who are less than sympathetic," the captain continued.

"But the Shoowa don't kill like that," Puck said. "The Grakk do."

The captain sighed. "Some people aren't so specific. They panic. To them a bemmie is a bemmie, no matter what. It's a pity that this incident got out. I would have preferred that the crew kept quiet."

"But it's not fair," Puck protested again.

"I know, Puck," Captain Biko said, reaching for a hand that Puck snatched away. "But he's safe."

"Can I see him?" Puck asked, refusing to look at her.

The captain spoke into her desk com, and a minute later a glum young woman showed up at the door. "Molly, could you please take Mz Goodfellow down to visit the brig?"

As Puck left, she glanced back to see the captain chewing a fingernail, unhappiness on her handsome dark face.

The brig was plain and much smaller than the guest

cabins. The couch took up a good deal of the area, and that was where Hush sat. His drooping head raised as she entered, and his eyes lit up.

"Puck, they are saying some think I killed." Distress trembled his voice. "I could not kill this human."

"I know you couldn't," she answered soothingly.

"I have disgrace," he said, his domed head bowing again. "That there are those who would be thinking I could kill."

"Hey," Puck said, sitting down beside him. "That's their problem, not yours."

"If it is being their problem," Hush asked, "why is it me being locked up?"

Puck tried to explain. "It's to protect you, the captain says." She couldn't keep the cynicism out of her voice.

Hush seemed to shrink into himself, his black robes swallowing him. "It is like one of those alien-monster vids you humans are fond of. I am almost wishing to go into deep sleep as Grakk prisoners do."

"We'll get it sorted out," Puck reassured him. "As soon as we dock on Aurora station, Michael's going to the port authorities before any evidence is smuggled off. They'll arrest Cubuk and get the truth out of him."

Hush shuddered. "Have you sure about Cubuk?"

"I saw the way he fights," she said. "And he threatened me. So why wouldn't he kill one of them to get all the loot?"

"Could it not have been the little weasel man, to be cheating his partner?"

Puck thought for a second. "I don't think he's strong enough to kill a big man that way, let alone drag him up through a trap door." *Leesa Sigmund,* Puck wondered. *Could she have done it? Nah.* It didn't seem likely.

"God. Another murder, Hush. Maybe we *should* warn the captain about Cubuk, so she can lock him up or something. I don't want anybody else killed." She tried not to think of what a smuggler might do to a man who was after her loot."

Hush touched Puck's hand lightly. "Then she will have the knowing you have found her secretness—this may be danger for you."

His words chilled her. "But what if she isn't a smuggler?" Puck said. "She'd protect us from Cubuk if I showed her that stolen treasure to prove our story, wouldn't she?"

"Do you think he had foolishness enough to leave that treasure in the crate? You will be having no evidence against him, and will be having him as an enemy."

Puck had to admit, it looked hopeless either way.

"The captain locked you up because of things Cubuk said he overheard. Do you think he put this into her head on purpose?"

"This is maybe," Hush said. "To some people, to be locked up gives a person guilt. They will not look for someone else to blame—the real killer." His face creased with misery and fear.

"But that's okay," Puck said, brightening up. "That means you're serving your purpose just sitting here. No one will harm you." Awkwardly she reached out and hugged him. "I'll be back soon," she said as she went to bang on the door.

But in the seconds before the door was opened she wondered whether Hush really was safe. What if Cubuk discovered the Soo was gone before they reached Aurora? He might try to make Hush tell where the Soo was, and there would be no way for the alien to escape. He was a captive, at the mercy of his enemy.

CHAPTER
TWENTY-ONE

That night they jumped again, and the next morning a message on the vidcom informed passengers that they were restricted to the lounge and passenger decks, unless escorted by a crew member who had notified the bridge.

Puck was fiddling with her grafix-screen in the lounge until Mz Florette spoke words that stopped her dead.

"Mizzer Cubuk. Welcome. How was your night?"

"Wonderful, thank you," he answered. "Interesting."

"What was it like up there?" Mz Dante asked, joining in. "Did you see anything?"

Puck looked up abruptly.

Cubuk laughed. "Well, to tell you the truth, all I saw was a swirling mass of gray. I guess I'll never make a hyperspace navigator. There were some odd noises, though," he added, and Puck's breath caught in her throat.

"Noises?" Mz Florette said, lisping slightly. She leaned forward in her seat.

"I didn't know one heard noises in hyperspace," added Mz Dante.

"Well, neither did I," answered Cubuk. "But there was the most hideous howling going on. The captain said I must be imagining things, and young Michael said he didn't hear anything either, but . . ."

"But what?" Mz Florette asked hungrily.

"Well, I had to ask him several times, before he heard what I said." He froze Puck with a direct blue stare. "That's odd, isn't it?"

Puck bit her lip. "You were on the bridge during the jump, then?" she asked.

"Yes." He smiled wryly. "And I certainly learned a lot."

Oh, God, Puck thought. *He's figured it out.*

"I understand the drive comes from the Grakk," he continued. "Maybe your friend knows something about those sounds since he used to work for them. Maybe I should ask him."

"I wouldn't exactly call it working for them," she snapped. *I can't let him visit Hush,* she thought.

"No, of course not," he said, putting on a fine act of appearing sorry. "But you know what I mean."

"Do I?" she said.

He raised his eyebrows, and she heard Mz Florette making quiet disapproving sounds.

Mz Dante changed the topic of conversation. "It's awful about that creature," she said. "Who would have thought it—a killer in our midst." She shuddered. "And I was all for giving him a chance, too."

Mz Florette just snorted, as if she'd expected it all along, and Puck jumped up to protest. But Cubuk beat her to it. "Wait a minute, ladies, nothing's been proved."

Playing the neutral to the hilt, Puck thought. *It's going his way nicely.*

"He's an alien," said Mz Dante. "They aren't normal. They don't think like us."

Mz Florette glared at her friend. "Let us not talk about it."

Cubuk lowered himself into a chair. He sighed and stretched his long legs out in front of him as he slipped a magazine chip into a light-frame.

Puck watched him warily. How could she stop him if he decided to go to the brig?

The ladies went back to their quiet conversation, and soon they got up to leave, cooing their good-byes. As they passed, Mz Florette paused and took something out of her voluminous purse. "Is this from that toy of yours?" she asked, handing Puck a crumpled piece of paper. "I found it on the floor." She didn't wait for an answer.

Puck smoothed the paper out. It was the picture of the Soo. Risking a glance at Cubuk to make sure he wasn't watching, she hastily shoved it down the nearest disposal. What a time for that woman to choose.

It was ages until Cubuk laid the reader down and rose to his feet. Puck followed him out of the lounge in time to see him entering the passenger lift. She didn't really want to, but she ran for it and slid in with him. "Going up?" she asked, sounding cockier than she felt.

"No, down to the passenger deck," he answered. "And you'd better be too. You know the captain's orders."

At her room she pretended to have difficulty with the

lock so that she could be sure he went into his cabin, then she sat in the corridor, where she could watch his door. She wondered how she was going to pull off following him again. It would look really obvious. *And what about when I need to sleep?* she thought. The situation seemed hopeless.

The freight lift opened, and Michael stepped out. He carried a light-board under his arm. "What's recent?" he asked as he walked toward her.

Of course, she realized, *Michael can help.* She put a finger to her lips. "I'm on surveillance," she whispered. "Cubuk knows there's something going on. He heard the ghosts last night."

"Yeah," Michael agreed. "I figured as much. He kept on mentioning noises. You know what he said?" Michael crouched to be closer to her. "He said, 'Now I know what I'm missing.' And when I asked him what, he said, 'Nothing.' "

"I wonder if he's checked his hiding place yet?" she said.

"Maybe he did this morning," Michael answered. "I meant to come and warn you, but Ernest caught me getting off on this floor, and he grabbed me. He sent me right to bed, like a kid."

"I'm afraid Cubuk will go down to the brig," Puck said. "If he guesses the Soo is on the bridge, he'll want to know where, and Hush won't tell. Cubuk might hurt him."

"What about you?" Michael asked solemnly. "You're Hush's friend. Maybe he'll come after you."

A shock jolted through Puck. She couldn't give in to it.

"I shouldn't follow him around if I were you," Michael continued. "I don't think you should be alone with him."

"But I've got to keep an eye on him, so that I know what he's up to. You've got to help."

"Me?" Michael almost squeaked.

"Yes, you. Whether your captain is a smuggler or not, she's in danger from him too. You could help her."

"Guess we play it by ear, then," Michael said.

Puck was glad to hear the *we*. "What's he doing in there?" she wondered out loud.

"Probably sleeping," Michael said. "He was up all night, after all."

Puck groaned. "Great!" It might keep him in one place, but this could get really boring.

Michael seemed to read her thoughts. "I'm not due anywhere for a while," he said. "I'll keep you company." He sat down beside her. "You're gonna need a crew member with you if he goes anywhere but here or the lounge deck."

"More homework?" she asked, pointing at his lightboard.

Michael sighed. "Yeah." He flicked the board on, and the screen filled with incomprehensible hieroglyphiclike symbols. "It's calculations for maneuvers in hyperspace."

Puck began to have serious doubts about a career in space. "It looks tough," she said.

"The biggest problem is having to calculate on the spur of the moment," he explained. "Some navigators have biochip implants to increase their speed; some don't need them."

"Will you need one?"

"I'll have to see how I perform under pressure," he answered. His forehead creased.

"You're not too sure about this hyperspace stuff, are you?" she asked.

He stiffened as if he was about to deny it, but changed his mind. "You've got to let go of reality slightly. It's hard to do. Scary. Sometimes I'm afraid I won't get back."

She was amazed he'd admit to being afraid; she would never do that. "You can do it. I know you can," she said. "You're really smart."

She blushed furiously, but Michael just squeezed her arm. "Thanks, Puck. You're absolute zero."

Puck and Michael were playing a game on Puck's grafix-screen when they heard the whoosh of Cubuk's door. They scrambled to their feet, and Puck opened her door to make it look as if they were just leaving too. She slipped her grafix-screen inside.

"Hello, Mizzer Cubuk," Michael called as the man approached the freight lift.

Cubuk nodded at them.

"Come on," Michael said to Puck in a loud, cheerful voice. "You can help." He winked at her, grabbed her hand, and rushed her to the freight lift before the door closed.

"I seem to be seeing a lot of you today," Cubuk said to Puck, frowning.

"We're on an errand for Mizzer Ernest," Michael told him.

Puck noticed the panel was lit for the freight deck. *Cubuk's not allowed down there,* she thought, but Michael didn't challenge him.

The door opened, and all got off. Cubuk stood watching them, a mocking smile on his face.

"No need to detain you," Michael hinted. He opened a grid beside the lift and rummaged around. He pulled out a rotortool and passed his finger back and forth over the activator—nothing happened. "Needs fixing," he said.

Mizzer Cubuk raised an eyebrow, but he turned to go.

Michael flashed Puck a glimpse of the base of the tool where he'd detached the power cell. "Can I help you with anything?" he called after Cubuk.

"No, thank you," Cubuk said over his shoulder. "Just exercising."

"Can't you tell him he's not allowed down here?" Puck asked. "He's not accompanied."

Michael wrinkled his nose. "Captain's given him freedom of the ship."

I might have known, Puck thought. "Get out of here," she whispered. "So I can see what he's up to."

"I can't leave you down here alone with him."

"He won't know, will he, unless you stay too long and make him suspicious."

Michael waved his finger at her. "I'll be in the lounge. If you're not up in ten minutes, I'm coming to get you, and damn your plans." He stepped back into the lift and activated it. "Come on, let's take this up," he said loudly. The distinctive whoosh filled the air.

Now that Michael was gone, Puck didn't feel brave anymore, but she took a deep breath and forced herself to catch up with Cubuk.

Keeping to the shadows, she followed him as he stalked the deck as quiet as a cat. He examined all the bays and opened several panels in the core that she wouldn't have known were there. Something by a bulkhead caught his eye, and he scooped it up. But it was only a tool—a wrench.

Slowly he worked his way around the hold until he reached the bay that had led to the Soo. He stopped there, and his face creased in anger. Suddenly he cursed, hauled back, and flung the wrench. It crashed into the bay.

Puck flinched and cringed between some cables. *He knows the Soo is gone,* she thought, heart pounding. How long before he went after Hush—or her?

He continued on, and she pressed herself back into the shadows until he'd passed. What would he do now that he was this angry? She had to put him out of action until they reached Aurora.

She slipped off in the opposite direction, looking around frantically for an idea. Just when she was giving up all hope, she found the pad-suit storage closet where she'd borrowed the handlight.

Puck opened the hinged door carefully. In front of the racks of thick pale garments there was space for someone to stand, and the extra pads that lined the back of the door would probably make it almost soundproof. There was a small air vent in the ceiling and no door handle on the inside.

She left the door open; then, deliberately making her voice lower, she coughed. If he was looking for something; she'd give him something to find.

She dashed a few yards and slid under the overhang of some kind of instrument panel.

Cubuk came around the core warily. He glanced this way and that, then crouched outside the closet door.

Great, Puck thought, her fists clenching and reclenching. He was on her level now; she hoped it was dark enough so that he wouldn't see her. She was glad he wasn't carrying a light.

He stood up cautiously and checked behind the open door, then he peered into the closet. *Go on, have a good look,* she urged silently. For a moment he stubbornly ignored her wish, but then he stepped inside.

Puck rolled from her hiding place and ran to the closet. She slammed the door.

Muffled thumps sounded from the inside, and a strangled, angry voice. But no one would hear him unless they were right outside. He could stay there until the authorities came to get him. Puck leaned against the door and sighed.

When Puck saw Michael in the lounge, he was rushing off for his shift, and she had only enough time to give him the victory sign from her favorite vid show, *Star Rangers*. He looked relieved.

—

Dinner tasted like sawdust. Any minute she expected to hear an alarm. After the murder the captain was likely to tear the place apart if someone else was missing.

She was leaving the mess hall when a young tech stopped her. "Have you seen Mizzer Cubuk anywhere? The captain's looking for him."

Puck's heart thumped as she took the truth and rearranged it. "Yes, I saw him a little while ago. He was going into his cabin, yawning. He was up all night on the bridge, wasn't he? Lying down this late, he could be asleep all night, huh?"

"Could be." The woman winked at Puck. "Guess the captain dines alone. See ya."

That had been easier than Puck had dared hope.

In her cabin the message light blinked on the vidcom. Was this a note from Michael or had they allowed Hush to call her?

A series of glowing letters materialized above the grid.

I know you have it. If it is not back where you took it from by midnight, I will come to visit—and you will not like that.

Puck stared at the screen, aghast. This message hadn't been there before dinner, and Cubuk was still locked up. Who was it from? Had she trapped the wrong person?

CHAPTER
TWENTY-TWO

Puck shut down the screen with a trembling voice. "What am I going to do?" she whispered, close to tears.

She paced the room, back and forth. *I should have minded my own business,* she thought angrily. But then she pictured Hush's sad face. No, she could never have refused to help.

She couldn't spend the night in her cabin now. She had to find Michael; he would know where she could hide. But when she sent a call to Michael's room, there was no answer. He was probably still on the bridge. She'd think of an excuse to see him on the way.

The captain was bent over a display and didn't notice when Puck climbed the steps from the lift to deck level, but Mizzer Nast did. "Where is your escort, Mz Goodfellow?" he said crisply.

She tried to swallow the lump in her throat. "May I speak to Michael?" she asked, as boldly as she could.

"Mz Goodfellow," he answered. "Mizzer Tse is currently on duty."

"But he promised to lend me a vid. He forgot, and I've got nothing to do."

"There's a large selection of vids in the lounge," Nast said. "I suggest you look there. What's wrong with everyone today?" he grumbled. "First old ladies, then girls. Doesn't anyone pay attention to orders?"

The captain glanced up. "Mizzer Nast, make sure Mz Goodfellow gets safely to her cabin."

That's the last place I'll be safe, Puck thought miserably. *It's not so bad,* she comforted herself; *Michael's not here.* But Michael came out of a side door just as the lift was closing. He didn't even see her.

Mizzer Nast seemed as annoyed at having to escort her as Puck was at being escorted. He left her in her cabin with a curt order to "Stay put."

Puck had to think of another plan. She couldn't hide in the hull, that was where the thief would be looking for the Soo. She might bump right into him, empty-handed and alone. But maybe she could hide in Michael's cabin. Who would look for her there?

She decided to take the freight lift down to Engineering —there was less chance of running into anyone—but the moment she summoned it, Mz Dante rounded the corridor.

"And where do you think you're going, young lady?"

"I'm looking for Michael," Puck said, sticking her chin out defiantly.

"Without an escort?" Mz Dante exclaimed. "Mz Goodfellow, you must know by now what's happened on this ship. You should be locked up for your own good." She led Puck firmly back to her room.

Before Puck had a chance to sneak out again, another message appeared on her vidcom. It was from the captain.

Mz Goodfellow—you are confined to your cabin. Other passengers—for your protection, crew members will be posted on the passenger deck and in the lounge. THESE ARE THE ONLY AREAS IN WHICH YOU ARE ALLOWED. If you do not report in to one monitored area within a reasonable time after leaving the other, a search will be instituted. I do not want any needless searches, and I especially do not want to confine anyone else to their quarters.

Puck muttered a rude word. Curse that Dante woman.

She opened her door to see if there really was someone there. A chime sounded. Great! And a tech walked toward her cabin. "Need something?" he asked.

"Just checking your efficiency," she said, and ducked back in.

Of course, if she couldn't leave her room without someone seeing, then nobody could enter without being seen either. Unless there was another way in. She explored the cabin nervously, examining vents.

There was a knock, and Puck's mouth dried. "Who is it?"

"Leesa Sigmund," came a muffled reply.

With the tech outside, Puck supposed she was safe enough. She opened the door six inches and locked it into place.

"Hi," Mz Sigmund said, peering through the gap. "Can I come in?"

"No," Puck said hastily. She didn't care if the tech was leaning against the corridor wall listening, she still didn't know how Leesa Sigmund fit into this and she didn't want to be alone with her. "My room's a mess," she added.

There was a moment of silence as her lie hung in the air between them.

"You haven't seen Mizzer Cubuk, have you?" Leesa Sigmund asked finally.

Not another one, Puck thought guiltily. Why did they all ask her? Besides shutting him up in a closet, she hardly knew the man. "He was going into his cabin to take a nap the last time I saw him."

"That's funny," Mz Sigmund continued. "I knocked on his door and no one answered."

"Maybe he sleeps soundly," Puck suggested. Why was Leesa so worried?

Mz Sigmund glanced down. Podkayne was winding around her ankles. The woman crouched and stroked the cat. "You seem upset," she said softly, glancing back up at Puck. "Is it that . . ." She seemed to search for a gentler word and was unable to find one. "That murder? Do you want company?"

Puck shrugged. "No, I'm fine. Honest."

"Well, come on up to the lounge if you get lonely," Mz Sigmund said. "I'm inviting everyone to a marathon vid festival."

"Yeah, sure," Puck answered. "Thanks." Leesa obviously didn't know she was grounded.

Podkayne slid into the cabin, and Mz Sigmund laughed. "Looks like you've got a visitor after all."

Puck closed the door. "Whew!"

Podkayne chirped, as if answering.

Puck tried Michael again in case he'd returned to his cabin. No luck. *It's a pity he's not the guard,* she thought. *He could sneak me out of here.* She huddled on her couch, with Podkayne snuggled up in her arms, purring as if to comfort her. Time crawled by.

There was another knock at the door. Puck gasped. *For a ship of people who are supposed to be restricted, there's a lot of activity on this deck,* she thought angrily.

"Yoo-hoo!" came a familiar, thick, fruity voice.

"For crying out loud," Puck muttered. "What does she want?"

"Robin, dear, do you have a moment?" called Mz Florette.

Puck struggled off the couch to the sounds of Podkayne's complaints. *If she asks me if I've seen Cubuk, I'll scream,* Puck thought. "What can I help you with, Mz Florette?" she asked through the door.

"You young things are so good with machines," the elderly woman lisped. "I want to watch a story, and I cannot get that dratted thing in my room to work. Could you show me on yours?"

Puck sighed, and opened the door. "Aren't you watching vids in the lounge with the others?" she asked.

"Oh, they are watching a scary," she answered. "Dante likes them, but I do not."

Mz Florette stepped in, her perfume claiming the air as its own. The smell must have offended Podkayne's sensitive nose, because her mouth opened slightly in a panting expression, and her tail fluffed up like a pine tree. She spat at the woman and dashed past her, out of the cabin.

"Never liked the beasts," snapped Mz Florette, shutting the door hastily.

It seemed to be mutual.

Puck went over to the vidcom. "Here," she said, "it's not hard."

"Never mind that," said the old woman in a voice that suddenly lost its fruity tone.

"Huh?" Puck turned to face her.

"You have something of mine."

Shock threw everything into slow motion for Puck.

"I said, you have something of mine."

Mz Florette's facial paralysis seemed more pronounced, like an image out of a nightmare. Her words slurred.

Puck tried to get ahold of herself. "What do you mean?" she asked.

"You know perfectly well," the woman said harshly. The *c* in *perfectly* clicked like a trigger. "The Soo, girl, the Soo."

"What?" This couldn't be. She was a silly old woman.

Puck backed away, realizing there was nowhere to go. Mz Florette stood between her and the door.

"I know it is on the bridge somewhere," the woman said as she advanced on Puck. "Those pathetic voices are there. They follow it. That is why I had to get it off this deck."

She jumped forward, faster than Puck would have guessed, and grabbed. Puck slipped sideways, heart pounding.

"You put it there; you can get it back." The woman smashed her fist down on the vidcom stand, and the thick plastic cracked. She didn't look soft and fat anymore.

Puck shook. "What makes you think I know about this Soo?"

"Why, you creep about at night with that Shoon slime, you drop pictures like a well-lit trail, and you are friends with that boy who is always on the bridge. Who else would have taken it?"

I wish I hadn't meddled, Puck thought. *I wish I'd left it alone.* She wasn't a screamer, but she screamed anyway—the tech would hear.

"No use crying," Mz Florette said sweetly. "They have all gone away."

That didn't bear thinking about. Puck tried to dodge around to the door, but the couch was in the way. Mz Florette grabbed again, and didn't miss. Puck's shirt was clutched in plump white claws. Mz Florette pulled her close, and Puck was overwhelmed by a stench underlying

170

the heavy perfume. For a moment she froze and saw every detail of the wrinkled, stiff face in front of her. One earlobe looked melted around the earring it held. Puck remembered the earring she had found in the corridor, then Mz Florette wearing a turban and borrowing a plastiwelder. The face was theatrical plastic.

Puck spat at the woman like Podkayne had as she realized what the cat knew. Some spittle reached the woman's eyes. Mz Florette howled, let go, and staggered blindly, still blocking the way to the door.

It all fell together—the mask, the smell, the squat, round form, and the way those men were killed. Mz Florette was a Grakk.

Puck lunged for the bathroom.

The creature's eyes were clearing, and she came after Puck once more. Puck pulled the water-pick hose as far as it would go out the bathroom door and aimed for the eyes again. A clear jet of water hit the knobby hands that came up to shield them, and the Grakk shrieked with anger and pain.

Puck squeezed around her and raced for the door. She slapped it open and tumbled out—straight into the arms of Mz Dante, the character actress, the makeup expert.

They tangled. "Beat," the real woman cried as she tried to keep hold of Puck. "You promised not to hurt her."

Beat, Puck thought. It suited her better than Mz Florette. That name was too human.

Puck yanked an arm away. She was almost free. Then meaty paws grabbed her shoulders and held her firm.

"Do not move," said Beat. "Not if you value your life."

It was then Puck saw the tech sprawled on the corridor floor.

CHAPTER
TWENTY-THREE

"He's all right," Mz Dante said. "He'll come to later." She stood there in her conservative dark dress and pearls, as if discussing a slight mishap at a dinner party. "She'll get it for us, then?" the woman said to her partner.

"Yes. She has a little boyfriend who will bring her the package he was keeping safe for her," Beat answered. "I warned her we have another partner aboard. She will not turn us in if she does not know which direction revenge will come from."

Puck's mouth opened. The Grakk hadn't mentioned another partner. Beat's fingers dug into a nerve in Puck's neck, and the pain made her feel sick to her stomach. She understood and kept silent. The Grakk seemed to be staging a different play than the one Mz Dante was acting in.

"What about him?" Mz Dante asked, casting a nervous glance at the body on the ground. "What if someone comes?"

"Let us hide it, then," the Grakk snapped. Keeping a hand on Puck, she swooped down and grabbed the inert tech by the collar. With absolutely no effort at all, she pushed Puck in front of her down the hall and dragged the large man behind her.

Mz Dante hurried beside them, her face grim. "I don't

like this one bit," she said. "When he reports it, there'll be trouble."

"He did not see who hit him," said Beat. "I could not kill him, could I?"

"Of course not," Mz Dante exclaimed. "And if you hadn't hidden that blessed thing down in the hold, that alien wouldn't have killed the other man."

Beat snorted in disgust. "I told you, I had to move it farther away, in case that Shoowa heard the noise and realized what it meant."

Mz Dante sighed. "There you go, talking about noises again. You sound like some guilt-wracked psycho in one of my old vids—'it was the beating of his hideous heart.' "

Puck wished Mz Dante would shut up. The angrier Beat got, the harder she squeezed.

They reached the ladies' cabin. "Not here," said Mz Dante.

Beat opened the door. "We will toss him back out before he wakes." Once inside, the tech moaned as if he were waking up, and the Grakk did something with her fingers. His eyes shot open, then closed again in unconsciousness. "There is a spot a little higher that can kill you," Beat whispered to Puck viciously.

The place on Puck's neck where the Grakk had squeezed her raised in cold gooseflesh.

The room smelled dense and powdery. Something sparkled on the dresser: a jeweled goblet. Puck recognized it as coming from that crate. No wonder the Weasel appeared so desperate the last time she'd seen him. The treasure had disappeared along with his partner.

· "I thought I asked you to hide that," Mz Dante said. "Better still, get rid of it. That's just what we need right now, smugglers after us."

"It is mine," the Grakk hissed. "They stole it from the Grakk." She stuck a hand down the front of her flowery blouse and scratched vigorously.

"And how did the Grakk get it, then?" Mz Dante answered, observing her friend's actions with distaste.

Beat stopped her scratching and formed her hand slowly into a fist. She stared at Mz Dante ominously, not saying a word.

"Well, you needn't keep bringing the stuff out to admire," Mz Dante muttered sulkily.

"Let us take the lift, my dears," Beat said in an airy parody of her Mz Florette voice, and grabbed Puck's arm tight.

Held against the Grakk in the passenger lift, Puck was close enough to see the reason for the creature's wheezy breathing and slurred speech. The glint of a chemical air filter was visible beyond the Grakk's now carelessly open lips.

"Did you have to lock the lounge door?" Mz Dante said.

"They will think it only an accident," the Grakk answered. "And it keeps those people out of the way for now."

"I don't like this," Mz Dante said. "It just gets more and

more complicated. I don't know how you're going to get us out of this now. With all these strange goings-on, they'll be searching cabins next."

The Grakk let out a hiss of impatience. "Believe me. I have a plan."

The door opened onto the bridge, and Beat shifted her grip to Puck's shoulder again before Puck could break away and warn the crew. "Not a squeal out of you," she said, as she might to a troublemaking youngling of her own kind. A pain shot through Puck's shoulder and down her side. It left her gasping.

Beat nudged Mz Dante out of the lift.

"What are you doing?" Mz Dante asked frantically. "We agreed the girl would go alone to the bridge."

But the lift whooshed closed behind them, and Beat urged Puck up the steps to deck level. Puck glanced back to see Mz Dante following, obviously flustered.

Captain Biko, holding a light-board to her chest, was picking up a coffee mug with her other hand. Mz Sigmund stood beside her, anxiously twisting a strand of long hair. "I'll leave you to it, then," the captain said to Mizzer Ernest, and both women turned to leave. They saw the newcomers at the same time.

"This is starting to become annoying," the captain said. "But since I have some questions to ask Mz Goodfellow, I won't immediately have you escorted back to your quarters."

On the far side of the deck Mizzer Ernest looked over

from the panel he inspected with a young woman tech, shook his head, and went back to work. Swann observed from the navigator's chair, where he sat sipping from a mug. He suddenly frowned.

"Mz Sigmund seems to think you're nervous about something," the captain continued, addressing herself to Puck. "Is that why you're here?"

Before Puck could think of a safe answer, Michael came out of a door. "I'm leaving now," he announced to no one in particular, then saw them and stopped in surprise.

"Go ahead, Michael," the captain said. "Off with you."

"No, please stay, Michael," Beat purred. She extended her arm, flicked her wrist, and a small tube slid down from her sleeve into her hand.

"She's got a Haldeman!" Leesa Sigmund could barely choke it out.

"What have you done with Cubuk?" the captain said automatically, fear on her face.

"I do not understand you," answered the Grakk.

"Captain," Mizzer Ernest said, still unaware of the drama unfolding. "I'm getting a signal from beacon Alpha-Thirty-eight Aurora." The normality of his voice echoed in the thin, unreal air around Puck.

The captain turned. "Ernie . . ."

A ray of light shot from Beat's weapon, and the panel in front of Mizzer Ernest melted into sludge as he snatched back his hands. He whirled to face them, his mouth open in shock. The tech gaped at the smoldering board.

"Beat, you said no violence!" Mz Dante screeched.

Beat ignored her. "No, do not bother to send a distress call, please," she said as casually as if she were asking her hostess not to call a hovercab. "Everyone! Over here!" she barked.

When they didn't move right away, Beat squeezed Puck's shoulder. Puck squealed. Swann leapt, startled, from his seat and crossed the deck, forgetting to raise the force field behind him, leaving the Soo exposed. Mizzer Ernest's eyes were narrow and cold as he accompanied the tech over. Puck was miserable about being the bait.

Beat spun Puck around like a toy to face her and clamped her big fist down tight again. "Now, where is it?"

She couldn't give in without even trying to resist. "I don't know," Puck answered.

Pain shot through her.

"I don't know. I don't know. I don't know," she chanted, though her body told her to tell.

"Stop!" cried Michael. "I'll tell you."

Puck was appalled. "No!"

"But it's no longer secret," Mz Dante said, her voice high-pitched and frightened.

"It could never be a secret again, once we revealed ourselves to the girl," Beat said. "And that was the only way to get the Soo from the bridge."

"But how can we get away with ransoming it back now?"

"Ransom it back?" The Grakk snorted. "You humans are such dupes."

178

Mz Dante raised a hand to her cheek.

"What?" Mizzer Ernest turned to the captain, but she looked as confused as he.

Puck took a chance. "She's a Grakk."

Mz Sigmund shivered. "Impossible."

The tech swore.

"Very clever of you, Earthlet." Beat leered. "Boy, tell me where it is."

"What is this Soo, Michael?" the captain asked, gently and calmly.

"It's the thing that was stolen from Hush," Michael said.

"You'd better tell her," prompted the captain. "I think Hush will understand. He wouldn't want Puck hurt."

"It's over there." Michael nodded at the navigator's chair, and Puck's heart sank.

Mz Dante protested again. "You've lied all the time. Ever since I found you in that storm drain on Fortune. I saved your life."

"Are you in with me, or do you want to get over there with them?" the Grakk snarled.

Mz Dante saw her fellow humans looking at her with varied expressions of disgust and horror. "I had debts," she said to them. "They'd have gotten their stupid thing back."

"Traitor," Mz Sigmund whispered.

"Swann," said the Grakk. "Get it." She motioned with the Haldeman.

Owen Swann edged toward the navigator's chair, shaking uncontrollably. He climbed the steps of the dais, eased around the other side of the chair, and bent over to reach the compartment under the seat. Suddenly he yelped and snatched himself back. He gazed in terror at something over the seat, something Puck couldn't see.

"I can't," he wailed. "They won't let me." His hand shot forward and brushed the control panel.

The Grakk spat something alien, and the weapon she held spat too.

"No!" wailed Mz Dante.

Mz Sigmund shrieked, and a brilliant halo exploded around the navigator's chair. Owen collapsed.

Puck's eyes watered, and through black spots she saw the captain dive at Beat, followed by Ernest. The tech ran for the lift.

The alien loosed Puck's shoulder and raised a solid foot into the captain's stomach, driving her back into Ernest. Ernest stumbled, and the captain fell to the floor, surprise and pain on her face.

The alien twisted, and another ray streaked through space. The tech toppled, screaming in pain, and lay still at the top of the steps.

Everyone froze in stunned silence.

"You *can* turn that force field off, can you not?" the Grakk said to Michael.

Michael still stared at the place where Owen Swann had been standing moments before.

"You'd better get it," the captain said weakly, pulling herself to a sitting position. "Before anyone else is hurt."

Michael walked over to the navigator's chair, as if in a dream, and picked up Owen's key. He held it over a sensor, and the faint shimmer around the chair disappeared. He opened the storage pod under the seat and walked back with a familiar bundle.

"Give it to her," the Grakk said, indicating Mz Dante with her head.

Michael handed it over, and the woman took it with unsteady hands.

"I don't see how you're going to get away," Mizzer Ernest said with a ferocity Puck wouldn't have suspected.

"No, you would not," Beat agreed as she swaggered over to a wall of colored lights.

The Grakk lifted a panel and began to fiddle inside with one hand, keeping an eye on her prisoners all the while.

Someone do something, Puck begged silently. But she knew they wouldn't; Beat was too fast.

"What are you doing?" demanded the captain, still short of breath.

"You will see," the Grakk answered. She slapped the panel shut and rejoined Mz Dante. "Hand that thing over."

Mz Dante put the wrapped Soo into the Grakk's waiting arm. Puck flinched.

Beat must have seen her. "Did he tell you it was a sacred object?" she said. "A treasure of his people?"

Puck nodded miserably. "How did *you* know?"

"I was once commander-in-chief of Shoon," the Grakk answered. "I had heard the legend of the missing Soowa'asha, but I always thought some slave master had acquired it years ago. I did not expect to run across it in a human spaceport. The Shoowa will pay a great price to get such a relic back. They will be happy to hand over the new hyperskip to me."

"But what about the money?" Mz Dante said. "I need the money."

The Grakk twisted her plastic face into a sneer. "And give up the opportunity to take back the ship that was planned under my command? Give up rejoining my people and being hailed for my cunning? Shut up and join your fellow creatures," said the Grakk, waving the gun at her. "You are a fool."

Mz Dante's eyes opened wide as if she'd been struck. She didn't move for a second. Beat leveled the gun at her. "I am almost sorry to kill you, you have taught me much." The terrified woman hurried over to her own kind. There were tears on her face.

"I will be a defeated commander no longer," the Grakk growled, and shot a bolt of light toward the far wall. A rosette melted, the access to a hidden door now useless.

"Ah, how sad when they find me," said the Grakk, in her Mz Florette voice again. "The only survivor of a great disaster in space." She swiveled, fired, and the lock of the emergency stairs dissolved.

"What do you mean?" the captain asked, her voice urgent.

Beat smiled poisonously. "You remember how all those defeated Grakk ships seemed to blow up, sometimes taking their captors with them?" She stepped over the motionless body of the tech and down the steps to signal the lift. "Yes, a Grakk ship can be quickly and efficiently set to explode."

The lift doors opened, and she disappeared inside.

"Where's she going?" Leesa Sigmund cried.

"The lifeboat, I bet," said Mizzer Ernest.

"Ernie, there's a stinger in my top desk drawer," called the captain. "Puck, keep on jabbing that sensi. We've got to catch the lift the moment it stops." She ran to the panel that the Grakk had opened.

"I can seal the airlock doors," said Michael, running in a different direction. "She won't get out."

But before Mizzer Ernest got back with the gun, a red light came on over the lift doors and a mechanical voice intoned, "Malfunction, malfunction, malfunction."

"Captain, the airlock won't respond," Michael called.

Leesa Sigmund beat on the lift doors with her fists, but the doors wouldn't budge.

They were trapped on a flying bomb.

CHAPTER
TWENTY-FOUR

The captain examined the guts of the control panel, shaking her head. "I don't know what that Grakk's done," she said. "I've never seen anything like it."

"All internal communications are out," said Mizzer Ernest, shaking his wristie futilely.

Leesa Sigmund paced frantically up and down, biting her nails. Finally she paused in front of Puck. "Cubuk is down there somewhere," she said. "He'll stop her. He's a detective with Interplanetary."

Puck couldn't believe what she'd heard. "What? He's a cop?" she squeaked. "How do you know?"

"I'm a news-vid reporter," Mz Sigmund answered. "I've been on the police beat for three years. I was dying to find out what he was up to on this ship."

Oh, my God, Puck thought. *I've trapped someone on our side.*

"I'm sorry, Puck," Mz Sigmund said. "When you acted so strangely when I came to visit you, I thought you might know something about Cubuk's disappearance. That's why I came to see the captain. Now I know the Grakk must have been in there with you, you poor thing."

Oh, scuzz, Puck thought. *You were right the first time.* But had Leesa told the captain Cubuk was a cop?

Mizzer Ernest muttered as he tried to pry open the

emergency door with a metal tool. He was getting nowhere.

Michael was kneeling beside Owen Swann.

"I'm all right. I'm all right," Owen said weakly, groping for Michael's arm to help himself up off the floor. "It'll pass." He crashed blindly into an instrument deck as Michael tried to lead him to a seat.

At least he's alive, Puck thought. The ray had hit the force field, not him; it was the flashback that had knocked him out. She wasn't sure about the tech, however. Mizzer Ernest had applied a thick layer of wound-seal from an emergency kit and covered her with a blanket. "She'll be all right if we get her down to the cryogenic unit in sick bay soon," he announced, but during his whispered conference with the captain his expression was grim.

Mz Dante, tall and deathly pale, whined a dirge to no one in particular. "How could she do this? I don't understand. It's not like her."

"Who do you think killed Sullivan?" Puck snapped.

"What do you mean?" Mz Dante cried.

"The last time I saw him alive, he was guarding that treasure she had hidden away in your cabin."

"No, the alien killed him. She told me. The alien thought that man had his statue."

"Beat is an alien, too, you stupid old woman," Puck yelled. "A Grakk. It's not who's an alien that matters." She stormed off, her heart pounding and her stomach sick.

Mz Dante and the Grakk must have been registered on

Cat's Cradle all along and had boarded early—they were the only ones without baggage in the lounge that first day —and that's why Hush had sensed the Soo was here when he was searching the docks. How could she and Hush have ever guessed that two old ladies were the criminals? /

"How long have we got?" called Mizzer Ernest.

"I don't know, Ernie, I really don't know." Sweat beaded on the captain's brow.

"They must have noticed something below by now," Mizzer Ernest said. "They'll send out a distress signal from the emergency com in Engineering."

The captain nodded and turned her attention back to the control panel. "It's a mess."

Hush could fix the ship, Puck knew. But he was as firmly locked away as Cubuk was. *I've got to set things right,* she thought. She circled the bridge restlessly, looking for ideas.

She had almost done a full circuit when she heard a familiar call—"Mrrrup!" She looked down to see the furry orange head of Harriman poke its way through a vent, right below where Mizzer Ernest perched on a control console trying to open the service exit.

"Captain," Puck called excitedly. "I can get out of here."

The captain turned. "What do you mean?"

Puck pointed to the cat door. "You can get the screws out, can't you?"

"But it's so small," said Mizzer Ernest.

"So am I," replied Puck.

"You can alert Engineering," said Captain Cat.

"No, I can get Hush," Puck explained. "He worked on Grakk ships. He's the one who disabled the space liner, for sweet's sake. He knows about ships."

The captain didn't waste time with questions. "Michael, get that tool kit," she ordered.

"But what about the Grakk?" asked Mz Sigmund. "She'll get away."

"Damn the Grakk," said the captain. "Let's save the ship first."

"The lifeboat hasn't left yet," said Mizzer Ernest. "We'd feel the vibration of its engines. She might be up to something else."

Puck hoped that whatever the Grakk was up to took a long time, because after she released Hush, she had to catch up and get the Soo back somehow.

"Try to find Cubuk, too," urged Leesa over the hum of the screws being loosened.

Puck felt herself blushing. She'd have to let him out.

The captain's eyes narrowed. "You do know something."

Leesa Sigmund darted forward, but Captain Biko grabbed her arm as the vent cover crashed to the floor. "Explanations later," the captain said. "We don't have time now. Just get to him, Puck."

The captain scribbled on her light-board and printed two sheets. "You'll need these," she said. "Give the note to the tech on guard duty."

Puck saw that the second sheet held a rough diagram of the decks. She shoved both pieces into her breast pocket and crouched on the floor to peer into the blackness. Harriman bumped against her left thigh, purring.

"Take this." Mizzer Ernest crouched beside her and offered her a small handlight. She took it, flashing him a nervous smile. The beam of light bit into the dark, revealing a platform and rungs.

Michael picked up Harriman so that he wouldn't follow her. "Be careful." The way he said that made her feel warm and brave.

The oblong of light above her slowly receded as she descended into the hollow exoskeleton of the ship. The wall began to curve inward after a while, and the rungs ended. She wasn't a cat who could jump from equipment box to pipe joint, so she shone her light down to see what she could do. The wall of the next deck bulged out again. She held the light in her teeth and lowered herself as far as she could, until she hung by her hands from the last rung on the wall of the bridge. Her feet swung in space. The way was built for adults—she couldn't reach the next set of rungs below. She would have to let go and drop a few feet.

Her pulse raced. What if she slipped? What if she went over backward and fell, ricocheting off etched walls to land injured, unconscious, or dead, wedged between some pipes at the bottom of the ship?

Well, then, the ship will blow up before anyone gets a chance to look for me, she thought, and that decided her. She let go, leaving her stomach behind.

She landed, scrabbled for a hold, and grabbed a rung.

Once the light was out of her mouth and into her hand, she spat out a few curse words and felt better. She checked the diagram and continued down.

She was outside the officers' quarters now and wondered if that was where she should get in. No, the passenger lift might be dead there, too, and she had no key to the emergency stairs.

She reached the widest part of the bulge, and the wall curved in once more. *I don't think I can face that jump again,* she thought. But here the rungs continued under, and she was able to follow them until she was hanging upside down as if on the monkey bars at school. Eventually she could carefully lower her legs and find a rung on the new wall below. This wall was more like a roof as it reached out into a larger curve. She flopped forward onto her belly, secured another handhold, and descended.

Now she was outside the recreation deck on the side where the lounge was. But it was useless to try there if the Grakk had locked the door. She'd have to climb down one more deck.

She didn't know how much time she had. The ship could explode any second. But she had to try. Hush didn't deserve to be locked away like a criminal when he could save himself—save them all.

Her hands were slick with sweat, and she dared not go

faster in case she slipped. The freight lift began on the next deck. Maybe the Grakk hadn't jammed it. Only that was the main freight deck where the escape pod was. She might run into Beat.

So Puck kept climbing down, and any moment she expected to feel the tremors of the escape pod leaving, or worse—the explosion that would kill them all.

Then she was in territory she recognized. She was outside the passenger deck. She clambered into the storage cabin.

Puck cracked the cabin door and peeked out. The corridor was empty, so she opened the door just wide enough to exit without activating the alarm chime. Who knows, she thought, Beat might have come back here for the treasure. A button on her breast pocket scraped the metal as she slid through, emitting a sharp squeak. She clutched it and cursed inwardly.

She hurried past the abandoned open door of her cabin and on toward the freight lift, her footsteps muffled by the carpet.

Just when she reached the lift, she was stopped in her tracks by a thin, intense voice. "I've been waiting for you."

She whirled.

It was the Weasel, as silent on the carpet as she, and he had a stinger aimed at her chest.

CHAPTER
TWENTY-FIVE

"What do you want?" Puck gasped.

"Don't be stupid," he said. "You know—the goods."

She bluffed innocence. "Goods?"

"You saw Sullivan bawl me out for bringin' that crate up day before yesterday, and that was chocolate I saw on the crate later—chocolate from the hands of a grubby kid. I've seen you sneakin' around. I know you pulled out all that stuff and skedaddled when you heard someone comin'. You must have come back for it later."

"Yeah, right. I suppose I killed Sullivan too," Puck said angrily.

He paused. She might as well tell some of the truth. "Yes, I saw your treasure—but that's not what I was looking for." She felt the sweat begin to soak her underarms and the cloth at the base of her spine. "But I know who has it."

"Who did you tell?"

Puck hated the way his hand shook when he said that. She wasn't eager to have her molecules rearranged. "I didn't tell anybody. She found it all by herself. It's on this deck."

His eyes lit up. "Show me—but if you're lyin', I swear . . ."

"You won't shoot me when I show you, will you?" Her voice wavered. If she died before she found Hush, they all died.

Maybe the Weasel felt sorry for her. They were both small. "If you can get the stuff back to me and not tell," he said, "I'll let you be. But if you tell . . ."

"Okay," she said. "It was that fat old Mz Florette."

The Weasel gawked at her in disbelief. "Pull the other leg, why don't you."

"They had financial difficulties," she answered, remembering what Mz Dante had said. "I'll show you," she insisted when he didn't stop shaking his head.

"Right," he said. "Your move." The stinger quivered in his hand as if he were scared of it himself.

Puck led him back up the corridor. She could feel a hot spot on her back where he trained the weapon. The door to her cabin was open wider. That must have been where he was hiding. She caught a glimpse of the mess inside. He'd searched the place.

She stopped outside the ladies' cabin. "In there." She touched the control plate. The door didn't open. "They're not inside," she prompted, hoping he knew what to do.

He grunted, fished a manual screwdriver from a deep leg pocket, and proceeded to pry the control plate off. She watched what he did carefully. There was a click, and the doors opened with a chime and the lights inside came up.

"Hutchins," he spat, and stepped back a pace.

Oh, scuzz! Forgot to warn him about the guard, Puck thought. She couldn't help smiling wickedly.

"Say, where are these old crows, anyway?" Suddenly the Weasel didn't like the idea of them showing up.

"Watching a vid," Puck lied. It was shorter than telling the truth. "It just started."

He relaxed slightly. "Wondered where Hutchins was." He stepped over the inert form. The door stayed jammed open. "What in the three worlds was they gonna do with him?"

Puck shrugged. "Old people are crazy."

He nodded, willing to accept that. "Jeez, old women. Who you gonna trust these days?"

Puck pointed to the goblet on the dresser, and he cursed in pleasure. "I don't know where the rest of the stuff is," she said, as he tossed the screwdriver onto the nearest couch and snatched up the bejeweled gold cup.

He wasn't paying attention to her, so she picked up the screwdriver and hastily slipped it into one of her own pockets. "Maybe there's more under the couches," she suggested.

"Yeah," he answered. He shoved the stinger into his waistband, pulled off a pillowcase, and dropped the goblet in. Puck edged toward the door, careful not to trip over the tech.

The Weasel chuckled when he opened up the cabinet under the farthest couch. She must have been right. While he was still distracted, she darted out of the cabin and used the screwdriver to reverse what he had done to the door. *I hope this works,* she thought.

The door began to close, and the chime rang. *Scuzz,* Puck thought.

The Weasel looked up, saw what she'd done, and dove across the cabin, grabbing for his weapon.

Puck ran for the lift.

There was a yell and a crash, and as the freight lift opened, she could hear a steady pounding. The Weasel was trapped.

But how much time had been wasted? How much time did she have left?

CHAPTER
TWENTY-SIX

Puck ran by the man at the engineering console and went straight to the brig. She handed the note to the guard on duty, and the color drained from the woman's face when she read it.

"What's wrong, Perez?" the man said, catching up with Puck.

Mz Perez unclipped a key disk from her belt. "Read that," she said, pointing at the note on her desk.

His eyes widened as he read. "Jeez," he said.

The prison door opened, and Puck shot through. Hush blinked in the stream of light.

"Mz Florette's a Grakk," Puck said. "She's set the ship to explode. Can you fix it?"

His hands flew to his face. "I should have been knowing from the smell," he said. Then his mind made several quick leaps and his voice rose. "She takes the Soo. She is getting away."

"No," Puck said. "Not yet. I won't let her."

"You are a child," Hush said. "Show me the where she went." He rose to his feet, towering above her.

Puck grabbed his arm. "The others, they're trapped on the bridge." She had to tilt her head back to look him in the face.

He avoided her eyes and tried to shake her off. "My honor. My task."

"The ship will explode," she pleaded. "Then what will your honor be worth? We'll all die. Even me," she added softly, afraid he didn't care anymore.

His eyes met hers, then lowered again, and his color darkened. "I am shamed. I mistake my honor." He paused, then spoke in a firmer voice. "I have need of tools."

Puck thought she'd faint with relief.

"I'll get them," the man said from the door.

"He'll need a laser cutter," Puck called after him.

Mz Perez joined them in the lift. "Akira," she said to her colleague. "Put in a distress call, then wake the boss." The door closed before the man could object.

Puck explained more as they went up.

"But what's taking the Grakk so long?" asked Mz Perez.

"I am thinking she is spending much time in the mending of the escape pod," Hush answered.

Suddenly Puck laughed, remembering how Hush had examined the pod in the cargo area. "You messed with it, didn't you?"

"I did," he admitted. "I could not be risking someone making a secret runaway. But she is being no fool about ships. She will have the seeing of the reason soon." His fingers undulated restlessly on the toolbox he clutched to his chest.

"Why don't they go into hyperspace?" said Mz Perez.

"The lifeboat can't leave in hyperspace. The lock doors won't open."

"They cannot until the meddling is undone," Hush said. "It is the hyperdrive that is excited to explode."

The lift stopped on the freight deck.

"Do not have worry," said Hush. "When we enter hyperspace, you will be knowing safe." He touched Puck's face gently, and she grabbed his fingers and squeezed.

"Gotta fetch the Space Patrol," she said, and gave them the *Star Rangers* victory sign as she left.

If I slam Cubuk hard with the news, she thought, *he'll be too busy to ask how I knew where to find him—until later.*

She pressed herself against the wall beside the closet, out of the range of a beam weapon. "It's me, Mizzer Cubuk," she called loudly, not sure if he could hear her through the thick pad-suits. "I'm opening the door." She carefully reached up and tripped the lock.

Nothing happened for a second or two, then the door swung outward. Slowly a shadowy figure emerged—Cubuk. A small sizzler glinted in his hand. The stink of scorched industrial fabric wafted out with him. He'd probably had to stop burning his way out before he smothered himself to death.

"What the blue hell is happening?" Cubuk growled.

She told him as fast as she could and had to repeat parts slowly as the words *Grakk* and *explode* sank in. "You're a cop," she said. "You can't let her get away." She didn't confuse him with the Soo. That was her job.

"Stay here," he said.

"No way," she answered.

"We've got words coming, young lady," he yelled as they both ran for the lift. He didn't waste those words in the short trip up.

The lift opened onto a view of the escape pod. Familiar moans filled the air, and a squat figure looked up from an open engine cover. "You," Beat spat, surprise on her green, froglike face. Her frilly clothes were awry, and the pinkish plastimask lay in shreds nearby.

Puck saw the Grakk raise her weapon, and ducked back into the lift. "Watch out!"

Cubuk fired. An answering ray melted a hole in the back of the lift, and Puck choked.

"Go back down," Cubuk yelled as he rolled out.

Puck heard a clang—the pod's engine cover closing, she suspected. Another ray crisped the door gasket. She heard Cubuk swear, and the hiss of his returning fire. Then there were engines firing, and a claxon warned of the airlock's release.

Oh, scuzz, Puck thought, springing from her corner. *Beat's fixed the engine.* The escape pod moved along the arc-shaped track toward the opening airlock. Beat was locked inside, and Cubuk swung from the pod door. He'd have to let go soon, or die when the airlock turned to vacuum.

"It's not fair," Puck cried.

Would the ghosts follow out into space? Could they keep up with the pod? Or would they be dispersed in its wake, to float forever in the stars—lost—never to find their way home?

Then Puck's feet left the ground.

"Hyperspace!" she screamed. Hush had made it to the bridge.

The escape pod ground to a halt as the lock doors closed, and the crackle of a speaker filled the deck. "Tell them to pull out of hyperspace, brat," Beat said. "Or I will melt it."

"Oh my God," Puck said.

"Melt what?" Cubuk asked as he swam toward her.

"I should do it anyway," growled the Grakk. "For the way you made me sweat. That Shoowa sabotaged this pod; a human would not have taken the risk. You got him out of the brig, did you not, little ship rodent? He was up there disarming my bomb all the time I was down here struggling with this piece of garbage. I could have collected my belongings and been gone by now."

"What's she talking about?" Cubuk insisted.

"The Soo. It's a religious statue. She stole it from Hush. If something happens to it, the Shoowa will be heartbroken."

It had more of an impact on Cubuk than she had expected. "By the three worlds, girl! Why didn't you tell anyone? Hush was under human care. We're responsible."

It was too complicated to explain, so she just shook her head.

"I am waiting for an answer," the alien voice croaked.

"There's a mike around front," Cubuk said. He kicked off from the side of the lift and pulled her with him. "What's that awful racket?" he mumbled as they skimmed across the deck. The ghosts, as usual, had gotten louder and louder in hyperspace until even less sensitive ears could hear them.

"The Soo is useless to me now that others know my plan." Beat's voice was oily. She was lying, Puck knew. She could still use the Soo. "When that airlock is open and I am halfway in, I will let you climb up here and take it, little creature. But only you." Puck didn't trust her one bit. The Grakk wouldn't even negotiate for the release of their own captured people; they didn't compromise.

"Can we stop her once she's inside the lock?" she asked Cubuk.

He shook his head. "Not once the lock procedure's initiated."

"Then we've got to stop her before that."

"We aren't in communication with the bridge," Cubuk yelled. "You fixed that. It'll take time."

"These pods have a rescue door in the rear," he whispered to Puck. "I think I can open this one."

"Listen," he said loudly to the Grakk. "I'll have to go up to the bridge in person to reason with them. I'll leave the kid down here as a hostage. Give me fifteen minutes."

"Ten," said the Grakk.

Cubuk lowered his voice again. "I don't know how well she can see out, so as far as you're concerned, I've left.

Talk to her. Keep her distracted." He pushed off and air-swam toward the lift.

And out the other side, Puck guessed, so he could creep around to the back of the pod without the Grakk seeing.

Now that no one was speaking, the air seemed full of the electric humming undercurrent of the ghosts. Talk to her, Cubuk had said. But what could she talk about? Puck reached for a cargo net to hold herself steady and remembered the unlikely place Mz Dante had said she'd met Beat.

"How did you get to Fortune?" she blurted out. "The Grakk never landed there."

There was no response, and Puck wondered if Beat was too busy keeping a lookout. The air was colder in hyperspace, and Puck shivered slightly. She caught movement out of the corner of her eye and tried not to look. Was that Cubuk or a ghost? Perhaps it was only shadows from the flickering lights.

The speaker crackled. "Why do you want to know?"

"It was very clever of you to be there," Puck said. "You must be very crafty."

"Do not humor me," the Grakk snapped. "It was not clever at all. When the humans invaded Shoon, I took one of the experimental hyperskips. But it was faulty, and I came out in Alpha Centauri with no fuel left. I landed badly on the first place I could."

"Didn't anyone see?" Puck asked.

"Fortune was evacuated."

Evacuated? Charon's casino moon must have still been shut down because of the war when Beat had landed there. "But how did Mz Dante find you, then?"

The Grakk hissed exasperation into the com. "You are too curious." But she answered anyway. "Antonia Dante found me eight Earth years later when she was walking home from a club too broke to hire a hovercab. I had woken from an extended hibernation and was digging myself out of a ditch."

"Didn't she scream and run?" Puck said.

The Grakk snorted amusement. "Antonia Dante has spent so long inside the skins and minds of monsters in her acting games, she has come to feel compassion for them. Her confidence was easily won."

Once started, Beat was apparently pleased to detail her brilliance, and Puck nodded and agreed dutifully so that the Grakk wouldn't stop talking and hear Cubuk trying to get in.

The ghosts were visible now. The translucent image of a Shoowa drifted across the front of the pod. Another curled around from below. More and more appeared in the quivering half-light. They slid around and across the pod like fumes. Sometimes she caught what sounded like words in Hush's tongue, words she couldn't translate but which scared her. They sounded angry.

Their faces were angry, too, and the air was cold and sharp. Puck remembered Mz Sigmund's scream. Could they hurt with their thoughts? What if Beat melted the

Soo? Would they strike out at all around in some nameless way?

Tears pricked her eyes. *Hurry up, Cubuk. Hurry up,* she thought.

Then off to her left the lift doors opened. Two bodies hurtled through the air: Nast to some pipes, Ernest to a bay. A blond head poked out for a look and ducked back inside. Mz Sigmund.

"I was expecting a peace party, not an assault team," crackled Beat's voice.

Oh God, they're going to scuzz it up, Puck thought.

"When are we coming out of hyperspace?" Beat asked, assuming the message delivered.

"Not any time soon, thanks to you," barked Nast.

Puck cringed. "No!" she yelled. "He didn't mean it."

"I am afraid he did," Beat answered. "And I cannot allow you to capture me alive."

"What the hell's that smoke?" Nast asked, then gasped.

Puck looked back in time to see the ghosts sucked into the pod as if it were a vacuum. Then the lights went out.

A scream came from inside.

Puck prayed that was Beat, not Cubuk. Blindly she kicked off for the pod and struck too hard, but she grabbed a rung before she rebounded.

The lights came up and the hatch above her head burst open. Two bodies rolled out, grappling and punching in mid-air like weightless cats. Each blow set off an exaggerated opposite reaction that sent the pair tumbling out of control in an odd, awkward ballet of mischance. They ricocheted off a bulwark. They slammed into the core. The officers left their cover and tried to part them. Nast was sent flying. Ernest caught a blow that propelled him to the ceiling. It was like trying to stop a whirlwind.

The Soo—Puck didn't see it. It must still be inside. She climbed into the pod.

The Soo lay uncovered on the floor of the pilot's cabin. It shot brilliant rays of color across the room, refracted by the twisting ghosts that danced around it humming a triumphant song. The phantom Shoowa looked fierce, not Hush-like. She was afraid of them, afraid to touch the Soo because of them. But she had to get it out of the pod. What if the Grakk won and came back?

She snatched the Soo up, her blood racing painfully through her veins, and the ghosts swirled around her, howling. One slid through her. It stabbed like a knife. She inhaled sharply and almost dropped the Soo.

"It's all right," she whispered, her voice trembling. "The Soo's going home. No one will harm it now." She tried to soothe them as she would a scared animal. "It's all right. It's all right." She shook, afraid of their sadness, afraid of their anger. What if they all sliced through her, would she die? "It's all right. It's all right," she crooned, knowing they didn't speak her language but willing them to understand.

Somehow they did. The noise subsided to an anxious hum. They stopped moving. Drawn faces watched her, layers of them, too many to count. They seemed solemn, wary.

The shouting outside ceased, and Puck peeked out.

It took all three men to restrain Beat, but Leesa Sigmund must have felt safe enough to come out of the lift. She held what Puck now realized was a vidcam in front of the captured alien as she awkwardly tried to stay in one place. Cubuk had a gash in his forehead; his face was bruised.

Puck carried the Soo out, the ghosts escorting her. Leesa Sigmund lowered her vidcam, a puzzled look on her face. When she saw Puck, she brought a hand quickly to her throat, causing her to drift sideways.

"I don't know what happened," Cubuk said. "The Grakk was about to turn a ray on that statue, when she suddenly shrieked."

It was the ghosts, Puck knew. They had cut through Beat with their anger, the same sharp cold that had stopped Owen from taking the Soo from the navigator's chair and had sliced through her in the pod.

"Her beam went wild and knocked my weapon out of my hand, so I had to jump her," Cubuk continued.

Beat noticed Puck—and the ghosts. "Get them away from me," she cried, dragging her captors backward.

Nast glanced at Ernest with an expression that said, "She's mad," but Leesa's face was white.

"Come on," Puck said, tired of the delay, bone tired of

everything. "Let's get up there and tell them to bring us out of hyperspace."

"That's not as easy as it sounds," Mizzer Nast announced bluntly.

Puck stared at him. "What do you mean?"

"Owen's blind," Leesa said. "Michael is navigating."

Mizzer Ernest cleared his throat. "And now he doesn't know where we are."

CHAPTER
TWENTY-SEVEN

Cubuk, aided by three techs, stayed behind to lock the Grakk up; Mizzer Ernest went to attend Hutchins, the guard Beat had knocked out; and Leesa Sigmund hurried to let her husband know she was safe. Only Puck and Mizzer Nast were greeted by the captain's sigh of relief as they tumbled out of the emergency door.

When Hush realized what Puck held, he kicked his legs into a joyous, double-bouncing swim that propelled him rapidly across the gravityless room. His eyes grew huge with pleasure as she placed the Soo in his arms. The ghosts had been invisible ever since she'd wrapped the Soo up, and now even their voices disappeared.

Mizzer Nast tersely told the captain what he'd seen.

"I feel like I've had the end of the story without the beginning," the captain said, staring directly at Puck. "I want to know what that package you gave Hush is and how you knew where to find Cubuk."

Puck's mouth dried.

"But not right now," the captain continued. "We've got other problems. Mizzer Nast," she ordered as Puck drew in a deep breath, "could you plot some alternate courses for real space? I don't know where we'll come out in the beacon field."

He nodded, straightened his cuffs, and set to work at a terminal.

"Has anyone seen Victor Zuzak?" Puck asked. She was puzzled that no one had mentioned finding the Weasel with all that treasure.

The captain raised an eyebrow. "Funny you should mention that. He was locked in with Hutchins. He shot from there like a bat out of hell when they got the door open."

"Did anyone go after him?" Puck asked.

"He's obviously not hurt if he could move that fast," the captain said. "We'll find out what his problem is later." She sat at a display panel and began to punch something into her light-board.

Was the captain afraid he'd give something away if he were caught?

Everyone on deck was hard at work.

Michael, tilted back in the navigator's chair, intently watched the domed screen above. Owen Swann perched on a stool to one side. Someone had tied a bandage around Owen's eyes, and Puck hurt for him. She carefully crossed the space between them.

Now that she saw Owen up close, his face appeared burnt. "Are you all right?" she asked.

"Yeah, thanks," he whispered. "Tell Michael *you're* all right. He can hear you if you put your hand on the chair arm where mine is." Puck placed her hand on a wafflelike grid, gently touching his so that he'd know she'd done it. "Go ahead," he said.

"Hi, Michael. What's recent?"

Michael glanced at her. "Hey, Puck. I'm really glad you're okay." The force field shimmered around him when he spoke.

"What happened?" Puck asked.

"I don't know," he answered. "I was going to skip back to beacon Beta-Ten Eridani, then forward again, as many times as we needed to. But everything looks different in the opposite direction."

Puck tipped her head back, and the sight took her breath away. They were gliding toward a smokelike misty-blue trail. Beyond towered a huge orange spiral. The colors made her tingle.

Owen groaned and rubbed his head. "It does look the same in the opposite direction," he said to Michael. "Only sort of inside out, not backward."

"But there was nothing like this green barbed-wire stuff going the other way," Michael said.

"Green?" Puck said. "That's blue mist."

Michael didn't take his eyes off the screen, but his eyebrows went up in surprise. "You can see?"

Puck laughed in amazement. "Yeah." Wow, she could see hyperspace.

"You're one of us," Owen said, giving her a brief but brilliant smile that warmed her to the core. She surveyed the deck proudly, but no one noticed.

The captain seemed strained and tired as she shot around the deck. She avoided looking up at the dome. Nast watched the captain with a worried and puzzled expression on his face. Hush hunched over the communications console, harnessed into working position so that he wouldn't float away. He kept the Soo in the double-jointed cradle of his left arm as he soldered circuits.

"Can't Hush help?" Puck asked Owen.

Owen shook his head. "Hyperspace navigation isn't a field he studied."

"I suppose he can't do everything," Puck muttered.

Mizzer Ernest returned to the bridge. "Got Hutchins to sick bay," he said wearily. "He'll be all right. Concussion." He strapped himself into a chair, and soon his eyes closed.

Puck was fascinated by the wildly colored contents of hyperspace. Her insides fizzled and popped in response to them, as if she were on a fairground ride. She was distracted again only when the captain loudly slapped her light-board onto a grip and propelled herself to the rest room.

Mizzer Nast pushed himself over to the screen the captain had been examining. His eyes widened, and he uttered something but quickly turned it into a cough. The sound must have worried Hush, because he joined Nast, and they conversed in urgent whispers.

Mizzer Nast abruptly stopped what he was saying when he saw Puck coming toward them. "Mz Goodfellow?"

"I've been in too much of this to be left out now," she said.

"She has truth," Hush agreed. "But, Puck, you must not be telling Michael. He must not feel pressure."

"It might panic him. Ruin any chance we have," Nast said, his hands clasped tightly away behind his back.

"What? Tell him what?" Puck urged frantically.

"There is different fuel for hyperspace travel," Hush explained. His gray face was solemn. "It is most expensive and is measured very exactly for each trip."

"We've taken a large detour," Mizzer Nast added.

"And it's almost gone," she finished for him.

He nodded brusquely. "The maneuver to get in and out of hyperspace uses up a great deal of that energy. If we fall below a certain level, there won't be enough to get out again."

Puck felt cold all over. What happened when you ran out of fuel in hyperspace? Did you drift until you starved to death, or did you suddenly fall? Where would you fall to? "Can't we get out now," she asked, "and worry about getting back from wherever we come out?"

"Hyperspace is shaped differently from normal space," Nast said. "We could emerge billions of light-years from anywhere we know. That would be worse."

Hush touched her shoulder, his voice gentle. "Our most chance is Michael will be finding the right way out."

Puck's eyes were drawn again to the swirling beauty around their ship—the insides of stars, the other side of creation. It was easier to believe it was only a piece of kinetic art up there, like O'Hara's moving walls that Gran had taken her to see at the Metropolitan, or one of Owen Swann's cubes.

"Yike!" she called out, and pushed off from the counter. She reached out for Owen as she passed and swung around to face him. "Owen. Your map. I saw that orange corkscrew on the map you were working on."

He grabbed her arm. "What corkscrew?"

"The nasty one we're heading for right now." Why had she said "nasty"?

"With a green cone going into its center?" Owen prompted.

She put her hand on the grid so that Michael could hear her. "I don't know," she answered. "It does seem greenish up top." And the greener it got, the angrier she became. She didn't understand.

"Michael," Owen said excitedly. "Puck sees what I see. Raise your angle slightly." He followed that with a string of numbers that sounded like gibberish to Puck.

Michael frowned, but he fed the numbers into a keyboard on the arm of his chair, then his fingers moved carefully over the pressure-sensitive control plate in front of him, dimpling its cushioned surface like water skimmers on a pond.

"Yes," Puck said as they sailed close to the outermost curl of the spiral. "There's something like a fuzzy whirlwind going up the center." She was so tense, the muscles in her back hurt.

"But I'm approaching a maze," Michael said, confused. "There's a black doorway ahead. I don't like the feel."

Owen cut him off. "Don't go through. Up!" he cried. "Over the top. It'll suck us in."

"There's a corridor to the right," Michael said.

"No, don't go around, whatever you do, there's a distortion field that'll rip us apart. Go over the top."

Michael's fingers scurried to comply, his eyes never leaving the screen. "I don't know if there is a top. No, wait a minute. Going over."

"There's wide-open space beyond?" Owen asked.

"Yes," Michael said. "Silver-green. Water rippling."

The anger drained out of Puck. "Rose sky," she whispered.

"Shot with gold," Owen added.

She didn't see the gold he remembered, but did he get this birthday cake feeling? she wondered.

"Stay on this course," Owen told Michael, and uttered a string of coordinates and degrees so fast that Puck wondered if he had a biochip implant.

"What's going on?" the captain asked, suddenly beside them.

Owen hushed her. "What do you see, Puck?" he asked.

"In the distance," Puck answered, "a long line of purple clouds."

"Ah," he said. "It's on the other side. I can feel it now, through your eyes." He gave Michael more directions.

Puck didn't bother to ask *what* was on the other side. It was something good, she knew. She glanced at Captain Biko and saw her back off carefully, a smile touching her face for the first time in hours.

"Do you see a hole?" Owen demanded as they approached the bank of blue-purple.

Puck couldn't see any break in the amorphous, churning mass. Fear crushed her hopes. "No, I don't see anything like that."

"There's a solid wall patterned with blue sparks," Michael said. His voice was strained. "I'll have to turn soon, or I won't have room."

The cloud mountain loomed over them now. Puck wondered what would happen if they crashed into it. Would they explode? Melt? Her heart pulsed in her throat. But was that a lighter patch against the purple? The hum of the ship around her echoed, and every whisper of those on deck was magnified. She understood now about the force field. She tried to block the distractions out.

"There's a light spot," she said. Something comforting nudged at her memory. "It's warm and salty." That seemed a ridiculous thing to say.

To her surprise Michael veered off toward the spot without directions. "Is this the way?" he asked. "I get a good feeling." His face was flushed, his eyes glittered.

"Yes, that's it."

"Go for it, Michael," Owen urged. "You're the pilot."

"And, anyway, we're running out of fuel," Puck said. Michael deserved to know.

Michael's eyes were wild with panic for a second, then he took a deep breath and accelerated. They shot for the bank of darkness, and Puck tensed against the shock.

The clouds smothered the screen, and they were lost in purple. Then the mist paled. It dissolved. They barreled down a tunnel of gray like the eye of a storm, and suddenly Puck had the taste of soup in her mouth—the wonderful chicken soup Gran fed her when she was sick.

"Hah!" Michael shouted.

Then they were out into another pink sky, with a spinning silver orb far to the right of the screen.

"I know this path," Michael said. "It leads to an energy flare." He pointed at the orb. "I can get us back."

Puck screamed and shook Owen joyfully.

The captain, Nast, Ernest, and Hush all faced the navigator's chair, their own work forgotten. Hush's arms were curiously raised, as if he gave thanks to a god.

Owen's face was white with exhaustion, but he beamed proudly. "You've got the nerve, Mike," he said. "You went with your instinct—that's what it's all about."

Puck gazed at the gloriousness of hyperspace. She had never thought she'd be good at anything, but this changed it all. Maybe if she worked really, really hard, she could make up all that math and science. More than anything in the universe, she wanted to be a hyperspace navigator.

Ten minutes later they burst into normal space, and gravity pressed down on them once again. They cheered like schoolmates winning the game, even Nast. The captain gave Mizzer Ernest a smacking kiss on the cheek, and he blushed furiously.

"You're a natural, Puck," Captain Biko said. "Anytime you want a recommendation to the academy, ask."

Then Cubuk came through the remains of the emergency door.

"Look what fell from the sky," he said, grinning. He dragged the Weasel in behind him and laid the pillowcase on the floor. "Bearing gifts," he added. An edge of cloth fell away from a sparkling rim. "I was checking the escape pod to make sure everything was secured when the gravity returned. He must have been hiding near the ceiling."

Now it hits the fan, Puck thought. Cubuk was going to bust the captain.

"If I'm goin' down, I'm not goin' alone," the Weasel cried. He pointed at Mizzer Ernest. "He's in on it. He stashed the loot in the hold and fiddled the cargo lists. Now what do you think of your precious second mate, Captain?"

To Puck's amazement the captain burst out laughing, then Ernest and Cubuk joined her.

CHAPTER
TWENTY-EIGHT

Puck lingered in front of the lounge viewport and watched the activity around the space station above Aurora. Workpods skimmed here and there like bees, and parties of suited welders climbed the sides of outer walls—insect mountain climbers, shooting bursts of almost invisible fire from their backpacks to boost them. Buffers ground out the Grakk insignia and shone the station into a bright new mirror for human and Shoowa alike.

Station security had already picked up Mz Dante and the Grakk, but they were keeping the arrests quiet for now so that they wouldn't spoil Cubuk's plans. And to Puck's relief and embarrassment, the captain wasn't a smuggler. She'd been helping Cubuk set up the real villains.

Cubuk had known the smugglers were desperate for a ship that wouldn't attract attention. He'd found out the name of the sleazy dive where the small-fry hung out from the man he'd fought at the spaceport—a man, Cubuk assured Puck, who was now a guest of the government Earthside, and not dead as she'd thought. Mizzer Ernest made that bar his second home. He pretended to drink too much and talked too loudly about needing money. Pretty soon someone offered him a deal. Mizzer Ernest sneaked their loot aboard; the captain pretended not to notice. Cubuk, traveling as a passenger, could keep an eye on the loot—see where it went and track down the big guys.

Puck felt so stupid. She'd gotten everything wrong and almost ruined Cubuk's operation. Luckily the Weasel was willing to cooperate rather than go to prison. He'd carry on as if nothing had happened, and the plan might still work.

"Make a great story, huh?" Mz Sigmund said, as if reading Puck's mind. "I can file it when Cubuk's captured the ringleaders. He's giving me an exclusive interview. I'm going to cover the Grakk trial as well. Two stories in one and me a witness. Absolute zero." She winked at Puck. "The shuttle's leaving soon. You'd better get going."

"I've got some things to figure out first," Puck answered.

"The ghosts?"

"Yeah." That was another story Leesa needed the end to, and Puck wasn't sure she could give her one.

—

Puck, Hush, Michael, and Owen Swann stood in the captain's cabin. Owen occasionally rubbed at his newly unbandaged eyes.

Podkayne and Harriman were curled up together on the captain's desk, Podkayne thoroughly washing Harriman's ears as if he were her kitten again and not a ginger tomcat twice her size.

"Let me get this straight," said Captain Biko, catching a mug that Harriman had been slowly pushing off the desk as he arched in contentment. "Even though there's a perfectly good shuttle, you want me to let Michael ferry Puck and Hush down planetside in the pod, using my expensive fuel, so that you can lure with you a bunch of invisible alien ghosts that I've never seen or heard."

"Plenty of people have heard them, Captain Cat," Michael pointed out.

"And seen them in hyper," Puck said. "You really don't want a haunted ship, do you?" she added. "It might be hard getting crew if word got around."

"I could always go into the tourist business," the captain said wryly. "Travel in the haunted spaceship—thrills, chills, and hyperjumps."

Puck's heart felt like lead. "Hush says they've got a strong connection with the pod since it's part of this ship," she told the captain. "They might shy away from an Earth-made shuttle."

Finally Hush spoke. "It would be a great kindness to my people if you are allowing this."

The captain's face softened. "And if the ghosts are invisible," she said, "how will you know when they are all boarded?"

Owen perked up. "That's my job. I can see them."

The captain rolled her eyes. "Why doesn't that come as

a big surprise? Go on with you. I'll let the surface know your flight plan."

"Yow!" Puck cried.

—

Puck checked the view screen and saw the captain and Mizzer Cubuk waving. They looked like puppets now, on a tiny stage. How quickly parts of your life became like vids that happened to someone else, she thought.

She sat down next to Hush and put her arm through his. The knobs of his extra joints were comforting and familiar. At least she'd have a friend down there.

Before he'd shut the hatch, Owen had guaranteed them that the pod was stuffed with ghosts. "We'll soon have them home," Puck reassured Hush. "No thanks to Beat."

"She had the want of being home with her people also," Hush said. "Maybe we have enough of likeness to be friends one day."

"I don't know how you can be that nice," Puck said.

"You are niceness too," he answered, surprised.

Puck laughed. "No, I'm not. I get everything wrong. My parents will be even angrier now that I want to be a hyperspace navigator after getting kicked out of school."

"I am thinking they will be much relieved," Hush answered.

The trip was too short. Before Puck had time to talk Michael into any acrobatics, they were landing. The pod slid slowly to a halt at the end of the runway. "Opening the hatch," Michael said, and the main door hissed.

It's time, Puck thought. *Time for all of us to go home—Hush, the ghosts, me.*

Hush held the Soo out to her. "You have the carrying of it," he said.

"No," she cried, startled. "That's your job. You bring it home."

Michael sighed with exasperation. "Well, one of you do it. There are people out there."

Puck swallowed nervously. "Let's both do it," she said, and Hush nodded a tremulous agreement.

"Wait." She reached for the Soo's wrappings. "It should go home pretty." She unwound the cloth until the Soo sparkled like a rainbow of stars.

At the open door Hush lowered the Soo into her waiting hands. He placed one of his own spindly hands on her opposite shoulder, the other he gently laid over her fingers.

"I'll stay awhile," Michael said, "to make sure all the ghosts leave." Puck looked back at him, and he grinned. "Next time we're here, Puck, maybe you can pod up for a visit."

"Yeah," she answered. Was that like a date? she wondered. "You nervous about your jump?"

He nodded. "Uh-huh! But I know I can do it now."

"I'm sure you'll be good enough until I come back to help with the maps," she said.

He gave her a mock salute. "Puck, you sure make life interesting."

She laughed.

"My friendship, Michael," Hush said. "Return in joy."

Puck and Hush carefully descended a disembarking ramp, blinking into the light of a new sun.

There was a group of people ahead on the dark runway and beyond them luxurious grasses that undulated like animals. Here and there a vivid splash of red spired above the green as if the planet were celebrating their arrival with fireworks. On the horizon, the brilliant blue sky was shot with a seam of rose. The air was warm, and clean, and delicious like honey.

Of the four people waiting a few meters ahead, all were Shoowa, except for one human in military-green coveralls.

Where were her parents?

There they were, way down the runway with two more soldiers. Her father moved forward, and one of the soldiers put a hand on his shoulder. Maybe the green-suits thought it polite to let the aliens go first. Her mother waved cheerily, so Puck decided not to worry.

Suddenly there was a rushing sound from behind, and Puck shivered in a cold wind. Two of the Shoowa fell to their knees, one with a bright featherlike headdress stepped back, and the human clapped a hand to his mouth.

Puck glanced over her shoulder. "Hush," she cried. "Look!"

He dropped his hands from her and turned as she did.

Streaming from the door they had left was an opalescent river, a transparent flowing traced with pale colors, as if the finest spun silk from a fairy tale were unwinding itself into the sky like a banner drawn to the sun.

She saw figures here and there with glugging throats and upraised arms, flying like ancient angels to heaven. And all around her were joyful cries she could barely hear, in a language she didn't know—sounds like the chiming of bells from the other side of a distant hill.

"Home, home," Hush chanted beside her, as if singing with them.

Far above, ragged shreds tore off, sparkled for a moment, then turned to mist and disappeared, until the whole bolt of ghost cloth was unfurled and gone, back into the life force of its own world.

Hush's throat vibrated so fast, Puck couldn't tell if he felt joy or pain. Maybe it was both. Her face was wet. She suddenly understood the color and shape of the precious object she held—life, hope, happiness, home.

They went to meet the stunned welcoming party, holding each other's hand. The Soo was buoyant in the crook of her arm, weightless as if it reached to the sun too. Still staring at the sky, the two Shoowa on their knees rose, brushing dirt from their clothes bright with colors she'd never seen Hush wear. One clutched tightly at an ornament attached to his belt and muttered as if saying a prayer. Her parents were too far away for Puck to see their expressions.

The Shoowa in the feathered headdress held out entwined fingers to Hush and said something to him questioningly. As Hush answered, he gently touched the offered fists with his own. One of the other Shoowa spoke quickly to the human, translating Puck guessed, but too softly for her to hear. The human appeared doubtful of what he was told.

She peered anxiously beyond them. Would her parents believe?

"Puck." She realized it wasn't the first time Hush had called her name.

"Sorry, what?"

"I would like you to be exchanging your name with that of this great woman of my people."

Puck gazed up at the alien woman with the feathered crown. She was taller than Hush, more finely elongated, and even more wrinkled. Perhaps she was older.

"Hushwa'shoonyashanyaha," Hush said, and touched the first of his three fingers to his nose. His name. Then he held out his clasped hands and gently crowned those of his waiting leader to show Puck what to do.

Puck handed Hush the Soo. "Robin Goodfellow," she said, and copied what Hush had done. The woman's delicate fingers were warm and soft. She glugged at Puck's touch.

"Chaiwa'shoonyashanyaha," the woman said, and fluttered her fingers up to each side of her long head, framing the display of her crown for a moment.

"Chai of the Asha people of Northern Shoon," Hush said. "Wearer of Wisdom. She is the leader of the Asha, keeper of beliefs, and the grandmother of my family still on Shoon."

Maybe I should have curtsied, thought Puck.

Hush held the Soo out to his queen. She took it carefully in slender hands, wearing what Puck now knew was a smile. Hush warbled something to her, then cast his eyes down. *He's telling the truth,* Puck thought. He didn't have to let her know he lost it, but he was anyway.

He said more, and the queen glanced at Puck. Puck couldn't read the alien woman's expression. The translator spoke rapidly to the Earthman, who occasionally also glanced at Puck in surprise. Puck hoped Hush wasn't going into too much detail. She wanted to sit down.

Then she noticed that Hush was glugging even faster than when he'd seen the ghosts disperse, and his shoulders shook with emotion. "Hush," she called up to him, and grabbed his bony arm again. "What's wrong?"

"She says . . ." He was having trouble talking. Were they angry with him? They didn't seem angry.

He started again. "She says it is to my honor that I cared so deeply for the Soo, but as important as it was to the keeping of our hope alive, it is only a picture of an idea and is not the idea itself." He took a deep breath. "She says they would never have turned their faces from me. I am the new hope welcomed home. I am the Child of the Asha."

Puck put her arm around him, as high as she could reach, and hugged. "Having you safe at home is the important thing."

The queen said something, and this time the translator spoke to Puck. "As our ancestors knew when they made the Soowa'asha, freedom is a child. Child of the Earth, thank you for being a friend to our son."

"You're welcome." Puck said, glancing shyly up at the queen.

Hush stroked Puck's hair. "We are children of the universe," he whispered. "We are all children together."

Puck wondered if he included Grakk in that statement; it would be just like him if he did.

"This reaches my hearts," the translator continued for the queen. "We have not trusted Earth. We have given you Grakk knowledge, but have not been willing to give the gift of ourselves. Now I cannot doubt that our peoples can be friends. You may tell your parents I give permission for their studies."

The soldier punched the air and grinned.

Puck stood there dumbfounded. Did that mean what she thought? She'd helped her parents out by coming?

"Go," Hush said, and gave her a gentle push. "Having you safe at home is the important thing." She saw him gently glugging laughter. "I shall tell them great things about you, so that they will never be angry at you again."

She burst out laughing too. "Fat chance," she said.

She waved to her parents. Her father stepped forward. When he wasn't stopped, he flung himself into a charge. Her mother dashed madly after him. They whooped with excitement like kids.

Wow, they're going to be pleased with me, Puck thought. She took off toward them, running as fast as she could.